UP FROM THE ASHES

THE RIDEAU CLUB STORY

CHARLES LYNCH

Published for
The Rideau Club
by University of Ottawa Press
Ottawa • London • Paris

© The Rideau Club, 1990
ISBN 0-7766-0310-8
Printed and bound in Canada

Canadian Cataloguing in Publication Data

Lynch, Charles, 1919-

Up from the ashes : the Rideau Club story

Includes bibliographical references.
ISBN 0-7766-0310-8

1. Rideau Club – History.   I. Title.
II. Title: The Rideau Club story.

HS2735.088R522 1990   367'.9713'84   C90-090389-9

UNIVERSITÉ   UNIVERSITY
D'OTTAWA   OF OTTAWA

The following publishers have generously given permission to use quotations from
copyrighted works: From *The Private Capital*, by Sandra Gwyn. Copyright 1984 by
R. & A. Gwyn Associates. Published by HarperCollinsPublishersLtd., Toronto. From *The
Canadian Establishment*, 1975 by Peter C. Newman. Reprinted with permission from
McClelland & Stewart. From "Farewell to the Rideau Club," by R.A.J. Phillips. Copyright
1980 by The Reader's Digest Association (Canada) Ltd. Reprinted by permission from the
July 1980 issue of *Reader's Digest*. From *Radical Mandarin: The Memoirs of Escott Reid*, by
Escott Reid. Published by University of Toronto Press, 1989. Reprinted by permission of
the University of Toronto Press. From *Ottawa, The Capital of Canada*, by Shirley Woods.
Copyright 1980 by Shirley Woods. Published by Doubleday Canada Ltd. Reprinted by
permission of Doubleday Canada Ltd.

Published for
The Rideau Club
by University of Ottawa Press

Contents

Foreword vii

Acknowledgements xi

Introduction: Not a Club Like the Others xiii

FIRE! 1

Nautical Elegance, Aloft 15

The Dear Old Place 31

Bytown Revisited 41

Dues and Don'ts 57

President Pearson 69

GG's and PM's 83

Who Needs a Club, Anyway? 91

That Old Diehard: Anti-Semitism 99

Dressing Up, and Down 117

Upstairs, Downstairs 123

"But Let the Women in Your Lives" 139

Appendix: Presidents of the Rideau Club 157

Foreword

*I*n early 1988, during the term of office of my distinguished predecessor, David W. Scott, with the 125th anniversary of the Rideau Club in 1990 fast approaching, the Board of Directors of the Club requested the House Committee to consider and report on the advisability of publishing an up-to-date history of the Club. The last history had been written by C.H. Little for the 100th anniversary of the Club and covered the period from its incorporation in 1865 up to 1965.

The House Committee appointed a sub-committee under the chairmanship of the late Dr Robert Hubbard, himself a well-known historian and author, and, in early 1989, this sub-committee brought a recommendation to the Board that one of our long-time members, Charles Lynch, be commissioned to undertake the writing of the history.

Having approved the recommendation and retained the services of Mr Lynch, the Board then approved the Committee's further recommendation that, to give full scope to the talents of the author, he should be asked not simply to write a dry, academic history but to tell "the story" of the Club from its inception until today in an accurate but lively way. I think you will agree that, in responding to the directive and to the challenge it presented, Charles has produced an immensely entertaining and readable account of our venerable Club's life.

To do this he overcame many difficulties, not the least of which was the paucity of available records due to the destruction of many of them in the fire of 1979. He made liberal use of those remaining, including fascinating minutes of meetings of directors and members dating back as far as 1867, and private memorabilia — to say nothing of the memories — of many of our older members and employees, and also had recourse to the National Archives and the libraries of the local newspapers.

I am confident that Charles's sometimes irreverent and colourful stories will be accepted in the good-natured spirit in which they are told. Counterbalancing these "fun" portions of the book are his insightful accounts of how the Rideau Club, a nationally recognized institution and one of the so-called "Town Clubs", responded to the societal demands concerning membership imposed by the modern views of human dignity and rights. As Charles has so graphically described, our Club has been in the forefront of numerous changes subsequently adopted by many other clubs throughout the country.

Finally, you should be made aware that, following the untimely death of Dr Hubbard shortly after the project got underway, our fellow member Liz Waddell did yeoman service in editing the original manuscript and liaising with the publisher, the University of Ottawa Press. Without her expertise the sub-committee and the Board would have been in dire straits. In furtherance of our desire to tell "the story" of the Rideau Club, Liz undertook to persuade the publisher not to subject the manuscript to the rigours of traditional scholarly editing so that the liveliness of our renowned author's familiar style could shine through in full flavour.

I am sure you will agree that the desire of the Board to give you "the story" of the Rideau Club has been truly fulfilled in *Up from the Ashes*. Happy reading!

John J. Urie
Ottawa
May 1990

Acknowledgements

*N*umerous people were involved in the preparation and publication of this book, and their contributions have been invaluable.

The enthusiasm of David Scott and the late Bob Hubbard initially gave substance to the idea of a new history of the Rideau Club. Subsequently, Jack Urie and his Board entrusted the continuance of the project to Liz Waddell, who was greatly assisted by John Scott.

As this was to be "the story" of the Club, rather than a conventional history, the personal reminiscences and memories of long-time members were needed to bring the text to life. Those who generously shared their memories and experiences include Denis Coolican, Tim and Pat Murray, Louis Rasminsky, Gordon Robertson, Roger Rowley and G. Hamilton Southam. Their recollections were complemented by the wealth of information found in C.H. Little's earlier history of the Club and by media accounts of Club events, particularly those of the *Ottawa Citizen*, the *Ottawa Journal* and the *Globe and Mail*.

The generosity of Yousuf Karsh and Malak in contributing their expertise also deserves mention.

The entire project could not have succeeded without the support and cooperation of the staff of the Club. Al Hofer, Maria Lengemann and Rupert Westmaas, especially, were unstinting with their time and unfailingly helpful.

Finally, the commitment and expertise of Toivo Roht, Pauline Johnston and Jenny Wilson of the University of Ottawa Press was of vital importance in the publication of *Up from the Ashes: The Rideau Club Story*.

Introduction

NOT A CLUB LIKE THE OTHERS

*I*n none of the many cities of
the world where they exist are town clubs famous for the
ardour of their commitment to progress and change. The
fact that the Rideau Club progressed and changed faster
than others of its kind, and survived as a consequence, was
due more to external forces than internal pressures. The
waves of change were felt strongly in Ottawa, and they
beat on the doors of the clubhouse facing Parliament Hill,
both before and after the government became the Club's
landlord and brandished the Canadian Charter of Rights in
the sometimes apoplectic faces of the aging membership.
As one writer put it before the changes, "Jews and women
knew they need not apply."

First to go was the blackball, the hidden method of
balloting which, for 100 years, had kept aspiring members
out of the Club. Some clubs across the land are still strug-
gling with this ancient prejudice. But the Rideau Club
abolished it in a glare of publicity that embarrassed the
Club and prominent members of the Jewish community
in equal measure.

Jews and women were not the only ones to suffer the forces of exclusion. Sandra Gwyn, in her marvellous book *The Private Capital*, tells of "a terrible foofaraw" at the turn-of-the-century Rideau Club when two federal cabinet ministers were blackballed. They were the Minister of Marine and Fisheries, Joseph Préfontaine, and the Minister of Inland Revenue, Louis Brodeur.

Opinions differ on what makes a good club, but there is agreement on one thing: It should be greater than the sum of its parts, whatever segments of society belong, or aspire to belong, to it.

It helps if a club is solvent and, after difficult times in the 1960s and 1970s and a spectacular rebirth in the 1980s, the Rideau Club is surely that.

Laments are heard that the Club is not what it used to be, yet if it were, it would be dead. The complaint that I remember best came from merchant prince Lawrence Freiman who, having braved and broken the blackball against Jewish members, later grumbled that "the old Club just isn't the same since they let women in." It was tongue in cheek, for Larry Freiman's love and respect for the fair sex was well known.

What the sum of the parts was, and what it is now, will emerge in the telling of the story. Once the most visible as well as the most famous club in Canada, the Rideau Club now cannot be seen at all, having exchanged clubhouse for penthouse. Some call it "Hy's in the Sky"

after the posh restaurant on the ground level of the
neighbouring tower — both are Big Business, with compa-
rable food and drink, and prices to match.

But a good club should be more than a watering hole
into which expense accounts and family treasures are
poured. If it should move and shake with the essence of
power of its membership, then the Rideau Club fits the bill.
The Club numbers 300 Chief Executive Officers in its
membership, making its premises a power centre in official
Ottawa — a place to see and be seen, a bustling place
where 250 people lunch and dine each day, discussing deals
great and small, signing chits, obeying the Club rules about
jackets and ties for men and "suitable garb" for women, and
usually ignoring the old Club ban against talk about matters religious, political or sexual. Thirty-two current
Rideau Club members are entitled to wear the Order of
Canada.

The library is little used, the billiard room even less.
But the private rooms are heavily booked for parties and
business sessions. Every Wednesday, the Round Table
meets: one-time potentates in politics and the public
service gather for talk over a simple luncheon with house
wine, and usually a guest speaker. Pierre Trudeau first aired
his views on the Meech Lake Accord in this forum, pro-
voking spirited debate. Jack Pickersgill, a prominent
member of the group, refers jokingly to his fellows at lunch
as "the extinct volcanoes." By tradition, the publisher of

the *Ottawa Citizen* acts as treasurer of the group, paying the bill and collecting from those present.

Far from quiescent, those old bellies have a lot of fire in them yet and so do those of the young ones who now give the Club its vigour as an action centre in the nation's capital.

FIRE!

$\mathcal{I}$t is hard to imagine a more "clubbable" man than Roland Michener, the former Governor General of Canada. Then in his eightieth year, he was sitting having brown toast and tea in the spacious, gracious old lounge of the Rideau Club on the afternoon of October 23, 1979.

Through the big plate glass windows Mr Michener could see the lawns of Parliament. Perhaps he was reflecting on his years as Speaker of the House of Commons, the role of First Gentleman of Her Majesty's Canadian Realm, when his wife Norah set up a School of Manners to teach parliamentary spouses how to handle their knives and forks, and other niceties of etiquette and protocol.

It was around those lawns of Parliament that Mrs Michener had waged a one-woman fight for "my Roly", when Prime Minister John Diefenbaker failed to honour him after he lost his Toronto seat and along with it the Speaker's Chair in the election of 1962. Norah Michener's gutsy lobbying made no impression on Diefenbaker, but it struck a chord with Lester Pearson who, when he won the 1963 election, appointed Mr Michener High Commissioner to India and subsequently Governor General. Mr Michener may have reflected on these things as he sat alone with his tea and toast in the building that had been as much a part of Parliament as the Centre Block itself. The Dear Old Club, he called it, though some Prime Ministers, including Diefenbaker, Trudeau, and the then current Joe Clark, had shunned it.

The old clubhouse had seen a lot of the nation's history, had been part of much of it, but it would see no more, and His Excellency Roland Michener would be the last to know its hospitality. In a few minutes he planned to leave for the National Press Club, the Rideau Club's raffish neighbour west along Wellington Street, where he would chair a meeting of the committee administering the Michener Journalism Awards, one of the monuments to the tenure of the Micheners at Rideau Hall. That done, Mr Michener would return to Toronto.

Bartender Philip Sylvain interrupted Mr Michener's reverie over an unread newspaper and begged His Excellency's pardon. It seemed smoke had been detected downstairs. "Sir," he said, "it might be well to leave the Club as there may be a slight fire."

Below stairs, the Club's assistant chef, Raymond Paquette, tried to telephone the fire department but the phones were dead. He ran next door to the United States Embassy but no one answered the doorbell.

Paquette raced around the corner to a Sparks Street clothing store and put in the alarm, returning to the Club to change from his chef's uniform into street clothes.

Upstairs, with a final sip of tea and bite of toast, the Club's last guest descended the grand staircase with his usual bouncy step, was helped into his overcoat by hall porter Ray Agrawala, and walked a brisk block to the National Press Club. Roland Michener had detected only the faintest sign of smoke, but when he arrived at the Press Club, he caused a late-afternoon commotion by remarking that the Rideau Club appeared to be on fire.

Press Club members poured into the street and joined fellow journalists who were flocking down from the Parliamentary Press Gallery on the Hill. Early arrivals were able to enter the Rideau Club building and wander through it seeking the source of the smoke. Some objected when firemen warned them that the whole place was about to go up, and ordered them out.

Go up it did! The crackle and the roar could be heard for blocks around, the smoke filling the sky and the flames reflecting from the surrounding windows of the Parliament Buildings, the heat so great it cracked the glass in the Prime Minister's office.

CTV's Craig Oliver achieved a small measure of media immortality by shouting: "At last, a story I can understand!" as he watched the biggest fire in the heart of the capital since Parliament itself burned down in 1916.

Coverage of the Rideau Club fire went around the world that night in story and news photos. The stories explained the unique role the Rideau Club had played in the life of Canada's capital.

The Club's neighbours were the United States Embassy to the west and, to the east, the 89-year-old Langevin Block, housing the offices of the Prime Minister and the Privy Council. Both buildings were evacuated and, from street-wide tongues of flame, the roof of the Langevin Block caught fire, despite the 750 gallons of water a minute being poured onto it by firefighters. Damage to the Langevin Block totalled $500,000 and Prime Minister Joe Clark's work was disrupted for weeks. Jean Pigott, one of Clark's top aides, reported that her well-known cookie jar was emptied by raiding firemen. "At least," said Mrs Pigott, finding the silver lining, "I'll finally get my office painted."

In addition to 60 firemen trying to control the blaze, there were 50 policemen trying to control the traffic and keep an estimated 6,000 spectators at a safe distance across the street on the lawns of Parliament Hill. The *Ottawa Journal* had 11 reporters on the story, plus its editor and publisher.

Up in flames went everything the Club possessed, save some crockery and flatware, and $12,000 worth of spirits and wine. Gone were paintings worth $100,000, including two A.Y. Jacksons stored in the basement. The Club had just completed a $400,000 renovation program to brighten the interior. Now, all was gone! Writer R.A.J. Phillips, in an obituary piece in *Reader's Digest*, mourned the passing of "a mark of power and a signature to the portrait of Parliament . . . a part of Canada's yesterday."

Also destroyed in the fire was the Tourist Reception Centre of the National Capital Commission, positioned to serve the swarms of visitors that make Parliament Hill the nation's second greatest tourist attraction, after Niagara Falls. The Commission lost tons of brochures, and a collection of antique tools used in the construction of the Rideau Canal, 150 years earlier.

Rideau Club men flocked to the scene and wept at the sight, though other spectators who despised the Rideau Club perhaps rejoiced at what seemed to be its demise. In the milling crowd I met a young man who had recently been removed from the Club's payroll, and his exultant comment to me was: "Served the bastards right."

With the heat of the flames in my face, I listened to the heartbreaking thuds as six of the finest Burroughs and Watts billiard tables toppled, one by one, from the third floor games room into the basement below. Against a crackling background, I gave TV interviewer Mike Duffy an impromptu history of the Club, later called the liveliest piece ever done about the place.

In the *Ottawa Journal*, columnist Doug Small wrote: "The Rideau Club, like many of its more notable members, is now a burnt-out shell. The fire in its belly is out."

Erik Nielsen, Public Works Minister in the Clark government, would soon order the blackened walls flattened, claiming them to be an eyesore. Nielsen had long regarded the Club as a haven for governing Grits, and he spoke with glee of its demise. Said he: "We drove them out of the provincial legislatures, then we drove them out of Parliament. Now we've burnt their club!"

Reports of the Club's death turned out to be premature. The fire put new life into an institution that would emerge from the rubble vastly changed but spectacularly solvent. This was a time, though, for reflection on what the Club had been and what the nation's premier town club had meant to so many movers and shakers since Sir John A. Macdonald founded it two years before he fathered Canada.

Wrote the *Globe and Mail*, October 24, 1979:

Few kitchens in Canada could turn out a better boiled potato or bread pudding. . . .

There were few scandals in the Rideau Club's history. . . . But it does have an anecdote or two in its past, the day an Exchequer Court judge broke a plaster bust of the Marquess of Lorne with a frozen turkey, and the night an 84-year-old member, who had a room upstairs, was caught in an ascending elevator in the company of a woman. . . .

[T]he old place was a piece of ourselves, with flaws, as well as virtues, that were come by honestly.

And this, in an *Ottawa Journal* editorial:

It has been easy to caricature the Rideau Club for a perceived pomposity, for male (and, at one time, Anglo-

Saxon) exclusivity, for a Victorian veneer which may
seem faintly ridiculous at the end of the 20th century. . . .
The Rideau Club did represent a style of living, a sense
of companionship, a gentility . . . which only fools
dismiss with contempt. It is much easier to call this style
elitist than to offer a better code. . . . Whatever the
public image, the Rideau Club was never close to the
stuffiness of an English club. It was a place of lively
conversation, of good fellowship, as well as good billiards
and good poker. . . . Above all, this has been an Ottawa
club serving Ottawa members, a minority of whom
hav[e] roles in government or politics . . . a place of some
civilization and ease where the very atmosphere seemed
to bring out some perhaps old-fashioned, graceful virtues
which made life seem a little richer, even a little more
humane.

The day after the fire, columnist Christopher Young
wrote in the *Ottawa Citizen*: "Many other Ottawans who
cared not at all for the Rideau Club as a club cared a lot
about the building. It presented an elegant, finely propor-
tioned but unobtrusive facade that stared steadily across
Wellington Street, decade after decade, towards the Parliament of Canada."

When the great fire was over, there remained only the
four once-white terra cotta walls, now streaked with smoke
and soot, enclosing a vast mound of rubble that covered
the ashes of all the Club had contained, including the
dozens of paintings, the trophies, the red leather chairs, the
racks of billiard cues, the huge grandfather clock, the bust
of Sir John A. Macdonald, the linen, most of the silver-
ware, and a century of memories.

The idea of reconstruction was barely considered in the wake of the fire. Lesser historic buildings had been restored after fires, but preservationists were not big boosters of what were deemed to be elite clubs. Had the Rideau Club been a refuge for the oppressed, or even a jail, the building would have been a sure candidate for restoration; as it was, demolition was indicated.

U.S. President Jimmy Carter was about to visit Ottawa, and the unsightly shell of the Rideau Club was deemed to be a hazard to his safety, since the United States Embassy was next door to the ruin.

The aforementioned irreverent Public Works Minister, The Honourable Erik Nielsen, summoned the wreckers with what some Club members regarded as unseemly relish and that, in clouds of dust, was the end of it. Some china, some tableware, a couple of prints, and a blackened Eskimo carving were all that was salvaged, along with the Club crest that had adorned the face of the building and the bottles of wine and liquors that were found floating in a luckily uncrushed basement storage room.

The salvaged wines themselves have a story that bears telling, but the tale needs this bit of background first.

Journalists have trouble mixing with the rest of society, be it high or low, because it is a tenet of the trade that it is better to be on the outside looking in than on the inside looking out. Better, that is, for the business of reporting and commenting, though inside tracks are important in picking up gossip and digging up dirt.

The problem is that, while savagery is practised at all levels of society, in journalism it is done out in the open, as a basic component of what media call "the product". Boardroom savagery, like that of the higher professions, is usually more subtle, and when blue blood is spilled, care is taken to avoid publicity.

So it is with clubs — in Britain, the "best" ones operate on the principle that journalists, by and large, are cads and bounders, best kept off the premises. When journalists form their own clubs, they tend to go broke, unless shored up financially by publicity agents and public relations people — their numbers make Ottawa's National Press Club one of the most solvent in the country, if not the world.

In Canada, media penetration of the city clubs has always included the proprietors of newspapers and latterly of radio and television stations. In the Rideau Club, the names of the *Citizen*'s Southams, and the *Journal*'s P.D. Ross, E. Norman and I. Norman Smith, and Grattan O'Leary have honoured places in the Club's annals, however much fellow members may have hectored them about the conduct of their newspapers.

In mid century the *Citizen* had as its editor Charles Woodsworth, son of the legendary J.S. Woodsworth, founding father of Canada's socialist CCF Party.

Woodsworth was his father's son, and swung the *Citizen* so
far to the left that it was referred to in the Rideau Club as
"the Pink Pamphlet". Woodsworth was fired without
explanation, and went on to a distinguished career in
diplomacy. At the paper, it was assumed a factor in the
firing was that the publisher was fed up with Rideau Club
barbs at his expense.

In a sense, publishers are like brewers — they cater to
the masses, but they move with the elite, never completely
comfortable in either milieu.

The old device of pseudonyms no longer works; moles
are sniffed out too quickly in our age of information. At the
turn of the century, Ottawa society reverberated to the
writings of Amaryllis, whose columns in Toronto's *Saturday
Night* chronicled the lives and loves of the prominent
without fear or favour. As Sandra Gwyn says in *The Private
Capital*, she had the "ability to make her victims quiver
with laughter even as she was leading them to the stake."
By concealing her identity, Amaryllis managed to keep her
place in society, and not until Ms Gwyn sniffed her out,
90 years later, was she revealed as Agnes Scott, member of
the redoubtable Scott family and forebear of assorted
Rideau Club members, including the father-and-son
Presidents, Cuthbert and David.

Ink-stained wretches who have been privileged to
acquire Club membership have tried to adhere to its laws,
written and unwritten, with varying degrees of success and

considerable unease. Sometimes, like converts, we go too far in efforts to conform, and my own most vivid collision with the laws of propriety came as a result of the fire that destroyed the Club.

As part of the Club renovations in the months before the fire, the wine list had been revised and a quantity of wine was auctioned, on condition that the bottles remain in the Club for private consumption. I acquired two cases of Pontet Canet 1969, and I had worked my delighted way through one case when the fire struck. I presumed sadly the rest were lost.

But the morning after the fire I got a phone call from Club Manager Al Hofer, informing me that the basement room containing the wines and liquors had suffered only a flooding and some heat, and that among the objects floating around were my bottles of Pontet Canet. I rushed over and, with the aid of the salvage corps, collared the 12 bottles, some with labels on, some without. Happy in my good fortune, I made my way back to the office contemplating my treasures.

I was congratulating myself when the phone rang; it was a fellow member of the Club, who came straight to the point. He understood I had salvaged 12 bottles of Pontet Canet. I agreed I had. He said that he, too, had some Pontet Canet stashed in that storeroom, so he assumed half the bottles I had salvaged were his.

What would a true Club colleague do?

11

I hesitated only a moment before inviting him over to get his six bottles.

In what seemed like 30 seconds, he was at my office door, swept up the bottles and was gone.

Upon reflection, I had second thoughts, especially having regard to the quality of the wine, one of the great vintages of our time, and always my particular favourite. I asked some colleagues if I had done right and they said I should have told him to go to hell. But those were journalists. I put the question to fellow Rideau Club members, hoping to be assured that a true clubman would have done as I had.

To a man, they laughed.

"He took you," they said.

One or two said yes, it was a true dilemma and there was something to be said on both sides. But not much. Possession was nine-tenths of the law; I had had it and I had let it go. Six bottles of the best. The incident still rankles, and I think of it every time I sight a bottle of the precious Pontet Canet, now priced well out of my reach.

One man, hearing of my experience, kindly offered me a bottle of Pontet Canet 1924, which he had in his cellar as a collector's item. I accepted, picked up the bottle and after contemplating it for a week, opened it. Sadly, it had spoiled.

But let us return to the Club, its shell levelled so as not to spoil President Carter's view. At the last moment, the

Carter visit was cancelled because of the Iranian seizure of the U.S. Embassy in Teheran.

For the Rideau Club, already in decline, the fire seemed a death blow. In fact, it was the breath of a new life.

A few weeks after the fire the Club moved into former Prime Minister Bennett's luxurious suite at the Chateau Laurier. At the end of November the Rideau Club held the 1979 edition of its annual black tie dinner in these new quarters. The guest of honour that evening was Governor General Edward Schreyer. There was room for only 130 members, but as author Shirley Woods wrote, "all agreed that it was an excellent dinner."

What happened next was the most remarkable chapter in the history of this or any other club: a re-emergence, a rebirth and a transformation.

Gone with the flames was the concept of a home away from home, a sanctuary from worldly bustle and strife. What emerged from the ashes was a club with no cobwebs, and only a thin skin of traditions and prohibitions.

New members, men and their wives, women and their spouses, who had shunned the old place as too fusty and formal, came flocking once the new age was declared.

New decor, new food, new standards of service brought prosperity and a waiting list, almost entirely business and professional men and women, career-minded.

The Rideau Club had once been a major station on the political power network — now, in its new incarnation, it would be the old boys, and increasingly the young men and women of business, industry and the professions, who would be networking.

In a peripatetic society, non-resident memberships proliferated and the days when everybody in the Club knew everybody else were gone. Things threatened to become so impersonal at one stage that the Club enforced the rule that every function has to have at least one sponsoring member in attendance, to be held responsible. Exchange memberships with out-of-town clubs had to be curtailed because the flood of non-dues-paying visitors threatened to engulf the premises.

Increasingly, the Club rooms and often the entire premises are booked for power lunches and prestige dinners, in addition to the usual social parties, from weddings to wakes, all subject to review by the executive.

The Rideau Club has emerged as the most successful club in the land, though it bears little resemblance to what went before. The Club is become young again, and brash, and irreverent, and rich.

Nautical Elegance, Aloft

he Rideau Club pent-
house is one of the wonders of Ottawa, even though com-
paratively few people will ever see it and public visits are
not encouraged. Those who enter the premises invariably
insist on a tour and fill the air with expressions of amaze-
ment and delight.

After all, it is in an office building.

And after all, it is all on one floor — one which
used to be the executive floor of the Metropolitan Life
Insurance Company, with offices much like those of top
executives in corporate headquarters everywhere — posh,
but not breathtaking.

But the Rideau Club has erased the office ambience
entirely and replaced it with something that is hard to
describe — until architect Tim Murray chuckles and tells
you to think about the old luxury liners that set the global
standard for elegance between the wars and after —
especially the *France* and the *Queen Elizabeth 2*.

"We reasoned," he says, "that if they could generate
that kind of atmosphere in steel tubs with low ceilings, we
could do the same with the eight-foot ceilings they handed
us here."

So it is basically marine design that inspired the stunning entrance foyer, the broad corridors, the uncluttered spread of the public rooms, with all the services hidden, all structural supports buried in the walls. Decorative columns are given prominence to accentuate the height of the ceilings, which are fastened tight to the concrete above, with all ventilation hidden in long slits around the edges.

The decor is a mixture of robust and chintz: wild bursts of flowers and bows along the walls and on the chairs and sofas, antique fireplaces that work, dark panelling to provide an air of permanence and the merest hint of the old Club.

If, as Tim Murray says, it is all an illusion, it is a grand one. The combination of the Murray designs and the decor of Giovanni Mowinkel brought it off. Murray's instructions to Mowinkel were: "The architecture is set — you make it look better." Murray says, "If he'd misfired, we'd all have had to leave town. He hit it bang on."

He certainly did.

Mowinkel didn't simply drape the place with that astonishing chintz, which would never have been accepted in a male-only club; he clothed entire walls. Equally challenging was the veranda-like link between the lounge and the main dining room, both so evocative of the great salons aboard ship, with everybody dressed to the nines and orchestras playing. The Veranda Room commands a

The old Club

*(John Evans Photography
Ltd., Ottawa)*

Edgar Ritchie, Gordon Robertson, Arnold Smith, and Jules Léger on the verandah of the old Club
(© *August 3, 1973, Yousuf Karsh/Miller Comstock Inc.*)

The grand staircase of the old Club
(*John Evans Photography Ltd., Ottawa*)

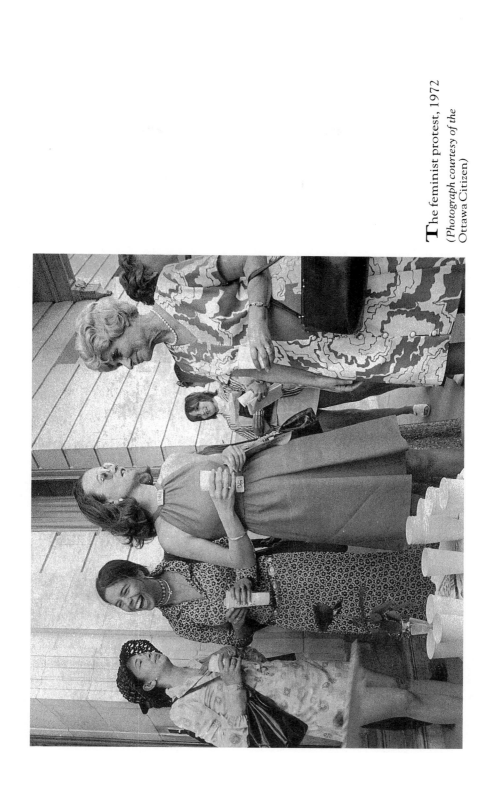

The feminist protest, 1972
(Photograph courtesy of the Ottawa Citizen)

The old Dining Room — a grand and stately place
(John Evans Photography Ltd., Ottawa)

⫶ MENU ⫶

OYSTERS

TURTLE   CONSOMME

BOILED SALMON--SAUCE BLONDE

FILLET OF BLACK BASS--SAUCE AU GRATIN

CHICKEN CUTLETS--ASPIC JELLY

MUSHROOMS--A LA CASSE-TOUS

ROAST SPRING LAMB--MINT SAUCE

FILLET OF BEEF--A L'ESPAGNOL

CHAMPAGNE PUNCH

QUAIL ON TOAST   PRAIRIE CHICKEN

SALAD

FRUIT JELLY   ICE PUDDING

SAVORY   CHEESE STRAWS

STRAWBERRIES AND CREAM   FRUITS

COFFEE

Dinner

to

His Excellency the Earl of Minto

Governor-General of Canada

9th March, 1899.

Given by

The President and Members Rideau Club

Ottawa.

President.

MR. JOHN CHRISTIE

Committee 1899=9.

MR. C. A. ELIOT   LIEUT.-COL. D. T. IRWIN

MR. ROBERT GILL   MR. J. TRAVERS LEWIS

MR. GEORGE F. HENDERSON   MR. W. LAKE MARLER

Sec'y=Treas.

MR. EDWARD WALDO

Dinner at the Rideau Club, 1899

"I think you're wrong, Senator — it doesn't seem to have anything to do with Sir John A.!"

Membership subscription receipt from 1895

Contractor's bill from 1889

A spectacular blaze
(Ottawa Citizen photograph by Ron Poling)

stunning view of Parliament Hill and environs, the Ottawa
River and the Gatineau Hills, beyond the curvatures of
Douglas Cardinal's Hull masterpiece, the Canadian
Museum of Civilization. Like every other room in the
Club, except for the bar and billiard room, the Veranda
Room is bright to a point that would make the clubmen of
old turn in their graves.

Mustiness and fustiness are nowhere to be found, and
the mood of high style and good cheer is sustained in the
paintings and prints that enliven the walls, replacing the
massive old oils that were consumed in the fire.

The broad corridors and circular foyer encourage
strolling, and the private rooms provide an intimacy that
has attracted paying patrons by day and night, accounting
for the Club's continued solvency. The most popular
private room in the Club is also the most spectacular —
the Board Room, lined with huge prints of the best-known
portraits of the famous by Yousuf Karsh, presented by Karsh
himself as a tribute to his beloved Club. The value of these
portraits is as great as the impact they make when you
enter the room, and it has been a humbling experience to
work on this book in the Board Room with the likes of
Margaret Atwood, Robertson Davies and Stephen Leacock
peering at me, while Winston Churchill glowered at
my back.

There are large rooms and small along the corridor
stretching from the newly named Lester B. Pearson

luncheon room at one end to the Sir John A. Macdonald Room at the other, all in close proximity to the kitchens that produce what must be the finest club fare anywhere in the land, served with the same quiet flair that makes the main Dining Room the attraction it is.

The Dining Room bears witness to the genius of lighting expert Phil Gabriel, whose instructions were to "make every woman ten years younger." Men are flattered too, and when you try to see how it is done you have the illusion that all the tables are individually lit, while in fact only the side tables are. It is the same sort of sleight of hand, or quality gimmick, that is used throughout the Club to such effect. The windows in the Dining Room are a mirage, too: a whole wall of Georgian glazing to hide the old office windows and create the ambience of a stately Rockcliffe home or perhaps the *Empress of Britain* or the *Queen Mary* in their seagoing pride. A ship high in the sky, giving its passengers one of the great Canadian landscape views 1,000 kilometres from salt water.

When it comes to deciding how to award credit for the Club's rebirth and rejuvenation, there is agreement on only two things: the expropriation, and the fire.

The expropriation proceedings were protracted and indecisive, and were only brought to a head by the fire, which was quick and brutal. But the resulting settlement by court order after the fire was as much a surprise to the Club as it was to the Crown.

It was on July 20, 1973, that the Minister of Public Works filed notice of intention to expropriate all of the three blocks facing the Houses of Parliament, including everything from Elgin Street in the east to Bank Street in the west, and between Wellington Street in the north and Sparks Street in the south. The notice promised an early appraisal of the Rideau Club premises, with the offer of a purchase price, adding that the Club was at liberty to make its own appraisal and then negotiate.

The executive committee immediately discussed moving to space in the new Metropolitan Life building, or erecting a new Club building on another site. And a letter was sent to the Minister requesting that the Club premises be preserved as a historical site. Club records note an intervention by Mr I. Norman Smith, publisher of the *Ottawa Journal*, who felt it would be immensely harmful to the Club's image if it leaked out that the Club opposed, or even haggled about, the price. "The board must give members a feeling of being informed at all stages of the negotiations," he said, "but not necessarily by means of a news letter, since this form of information is too readily leaked to the press."

On January 10, 1974, the Club received notice that, effective December 28, 1973, the Rideau Club property had become the property of the Crown.

On March 14, 1974, President Ernest D. Lafferty tabled a letter from the Department of Public Works in which they offered to pay the Club $1,310,000, "in accordance with the terms of the expropriation." It was the opinion of the Club's expropriation committee that the amount was too small to constitute a valid offer.

Negotiations dragged on, amid private assurances that the Club could stay in the building for at least another decade, since plans to build a new South Block of Parliament on the site, to match the Centre Block and create a Parliamentary Quadrangle, had proven too expensive to contemplate.

The Club was subjected to unaccustomed and unwelcome publicity because of its exposed position, and President Lafferty reported that members were objecting to articles written by journalists Peter Newman and Christopher Young, both members of the Club. The records report considerable discussion, pro and con, followed by a Board decision that "no action should be taken at this time."

In 1976, the Club tried a negotiating ploy, with the Board of Directors openly discussing disposition of Club assets upon dissolution. The records put it this way: "It was tentatively agreed that a good solution would be to refund basic initiation fees with no appreciation allowed, and to donate the balance to charity. General knowledge of the Club's policy in this regard could help in our negotiations with the government."

The cat-and-mouse game ended with the fire and the Club emerged as a mouse that roared, developing a new drive for life that brought into play the talents of Tim and Pat Murray and Giovanni Mowinkel, who together created a masterpiece.

They had to have something to work with and, since the Club was in such decline when the fire struck, there might not have been much. In fact, there was $10.5 million, thanks to an expropriation award judgement of Mr Justice James Jerome in the Federal Court.

Those who presented the Club's case to Mr Justice Jerome played their persuasive part, countering all the arguments the government side brought forward to support an increased expropriation offer of $3 million.

The federal lawyers had claimed the old clubhouse was a heap of junk even before it burned, devoid of architectural or structural merit, a veritable eyesore on the face of Parliament.

The Club's reply, orchestrated by lawyer David Scott, Club President Stuart F.M. "Swatty" Wotherspoon, and architect Tim Murray, was that the real value of the old Club lay in its location and the fact that, having been there so many years, it "fitted in". Far from being irrelevant, that setting was worth a very substantial something.

The argument was that if you were doing a valuation of the Houses of Parliament, you wouldn't call them bad Gothic because they were not a cathedral. The Chateau

Laurier would not be damned because it was not a true Loire Valley chateau. And Ottawa's old Union Station, now the federal Conference Centre, would not be dismissed because, architecturally, it was a poor replica of Rome's Baths of Caracalla. Why, Judge Jerome was asked, devalue the Rideau Club building because of its indifferent, derivative design? Technologically sophisticated appraisals are all right as far as they go, but they ignore the human emotions a building can evoke. Was the Rideau Club not a much-loved building? The answer was evident: it was.

The Club produced evidence that views of the Imperial Palace in Tokyo added significant value to the properties around, including the Canadian Embassy, the most precious real estate jewel in Canada's international crown. In Washington, hotels with views of the White House charge premium rates. In Vancouver, the most magical word in the real estate business is "view". And in Ottawa, when the Royal Bank built its new tower just down the street from the Rideau Club, the floors that went first, and for the highest rents, were the top ones, with a view of Parliament Hill.

When Mr Justice Jerome questioned this line of argument, he was told that he was wrong. So Judge Jerome, adjudicating his first expropriation case, went back to the books, and his office became literally strewn with papers and graphs, diagrams and charts. This case had come to him because he was virtually the only Federal

Court judge in town who was not a member of the
Rideau Club.

I confess here to tampering with justice to this extent:
knowing that Judge Jerome was a fellow piano player and
pool shark, I suggested that, whatever his decision, it
should leave the Club with enough money for a new
billiard room.

"How many tables?" was his interested response.

"Four," said I.

The old Club had had six, but there were seldom
more than four in use at any one time.

The Club was expecting an award of $6.5 million,
taking into account the $750,000 the government had
advanced against the then undetermined expropriation
to pay for a cosmetic renovation of the old Club prior to
the fire.

The judgement was a complex one. Conditions had to
be met if the Club was to receive the full $10.5 million.
Members withheld their cheers until they could analyze the
terms fully. And their good fortune was still shadowed by
the possibility of an appeal by the government. In the end,
the government decided not to appeal, and so the Club
emerged with more money than its members had any
reason to expect.

While the lawyers reviewed the judgement, the search
for new premises began. Here, the heroes were the members of the Relocation Committee headed by James Ross,

the man who had been President when the clubhouse burned down and who had spearheaded the fast move to the big Chateau Laurier suite that had once been home to Prime Minister Richard Bedford Bennett. That move had preserved the Club's atmosphere but greatly diminished its space; now, the Club could soar again, provided the right place could be found.

To retain the full amount of the court award, it would be necessary for the Club to own any new premises outright, by purchase; renting would subject the capital amount to a punitive tax assessment.

But downtown Ottawa land prices in 1980 were such that a building for Club purposes only, say of two or three stories, was out of the question.

Where to go?

The top floor of the Skyline Hotel was looked at, but the kitchen it had once contained was gone. The floor was deemed to be too big anyway, and the hotel's location was on the edge of the city's centre, rather than in the middle.

The Chateau Laurier parking garage was a serious possibility, the idea being to build the Club premises on top of it to enjoy an unparalleled view of Parliament Hill and the river. No dice: too forbidding, and Ottawa parking garages all suffer structurally from salt rot, because the city douses its streets with 30,000 tons of metal-eating sodium chloride every winter.

The British High Commission was willing to sell the Club a couple of floors in its building on Confederation Square, since Her Majesty's Government was tightening up on foreign spending and could use the cash. But the premises lacked the desired view, and it was felt the red tape would take too long to unravel. (In the event, the High Commission converted its lower floors into commercial space, welcoming all comers.)

The Howard Johnson hotel on Slater Street was considered, and St Andrew's Church offered space in an office building then being planned — and subsequently erected — on the church's Kent Street property. Buying the Country Club in Hull was proposed, but even though the property was magnificent, this idea was rejected because it was out of town, too far from Parliament Hill. (The Country Club eventually subdivided its land and, with the proceeds, has entered on a new life of its own.)

The Metropolitan Life Insurance Company made repeated suggestions that the Club become a tenant in its new building at 99 Bank Street, erected after the government expropriated the original MetLife Building, now a block of the Parliamentary precinct itself.

A new building was planned behind the Royal Bank building, and the developers offered the Rideau Club its own wing. But, no view, no deal.

The American Embassy, beside the old clubhouse site, was considered, but rejected as being too small — apart from not being available.

The Birks Building, immediately south of the old clubhouse site, offered three floors, but by this time the Club was concentrating on a one-big-floor solution.

The government was asked to help, since, under the terms of the original expropriation, the Department of Public Works had made a commitment to help the Club relocate when the old clubhouse had to be vacated. But NCC Chairman Bud Drury, himself a member of the Rideau Club, was unenthusiastic, suggesting the Club make a deal with a developer and get on with it. In vain did the Club plead that its $1 million insurance policy on the old building carried a rider that required rebuilding on the old site. The government was adamant. There would be no rebuilding there, so out went the million.

Chairman Ross and his cohorts on the committee spread the word on the street that the Rideau Club was looking and that, following the Jerome judgement, it had the money.

Metropolitan Life now came through with a new offer: to sell, on a condominium basis, either the top floor of its existing building, or the second floor of a new building it was planning next door. Price: $5,500,000.

The space in the new building would have no view. The space atop the existing MetLife building provided a

panorama of the entire national capital area, as far as
Kingsmere to the north, and including at least a slice of
Parliament Hill, provided nobody put a highrise in
between.

The Club offered $5,200,000 for the floor with
the view.

A 30-day option was taken and extended by agreement with Metropolitan Life when the promoters of a new
building on the Sparks Street Mall offered premises that
would include as many as six squash courts.

Squash had often been proposed as a means of attracting younger members to the Club and arguments raged
about the propriety of the Rideau Club going into athletic
activities more strenuous than the wielding of cutlery or
crystal, billiard cues or decks of cards. The view that
carried the day was that squash players are not big spend-
ers. One member, himself a squash player, suggested the
squash player's lunch consisted of a dish of prunes and a
glass of water.

The developers of the Sparks Street building orga-
nized a lobby within the ranks of Rideau Club members
and the decision went to a general meeting where
speeches, as impassioned as any on the women's issue
(recounted in the last chapter of this book), rent the air.
In the end, the momentum was with the MetLife top
floor, again because it had the view and the other
contestants hadn't.

The decision was made to get on with the renovation plans atop what was then the most impressive office tower in town. The Club's architects, the Murray brothers, ignoring their distaste for eight-foot ceilings, had wrung from the building's owner permission to drive a hole in the ceiling to accommodate the foyer dome that is the principal glory of the new premises. The dome rises into what is, in effect, the building's attic, the Club claiming its one-fifteenth share of the airspace there. In that dome, designer Giovanni Mowinkel hung a $25,000 crystal chandelier he bought in England, and he and the Murrays proceeded enthusiastically with the rest of the work, all parties agreeing it was the most exciting commission any of them had ever had.

While this was going on, an uneasy membership continued to enjoy Club life on a small scale at the Chateau Laurier. Women members and guests said that they liked the Chateau suite, the service, and the food better than their equivalents in the old clubhouse, which they had found forbidding.

And when the new premises were opened, there was the billiard room, not with four tables, but with three. The walls, instead of being panelled as they might have been in a games room, were hung with the most striking possible examples of native art, including the famous Morrisseau print of an Indian man and woman indulging explicitly in the sex act (the one thing all visitors to the Club insist on

seeing and gasp when they do). As collector Hamilton
Southam put it, "if we couldn't get a nude over the bar, at
least we got that!"

There had been no room for the Club's coterie of
billiard and snooker players at the Chateau Laurier and it
had fallen to my lot to find them a temporary home. The
result was one of the most comical episodes in Club history
because it involved what became known as the mixing of
the toughs and toffs, the toughs carrying the day.

The place I found for the Rideau Club players was the
Century pool hall, which, for almost 100 years, had been
open for business at the corner of Sparks and Bank streets.
This venerable old relic boasted 12 tables on its main floor,
and two more on the floor above that were reserved by the
proprietor for the private enjoyment of favoured players in
the then-murky world of pool. The game has since become
as respectable as bowling, but this was when people in pool
halls were still smoking and cussing and hustling.

Arrangements were made for the Rideau Club players
to have access to the favoured tables on the top floor and
a date was set for our first visit to the premises, all proper
notices having been sent out and a scale of charges
agreed upon.

We arrived in a body, ascending the rickety wooden
stairs to the first floor, the main pool hall, with its snack
bar, spittoons and smoke. The regular crowd had assembled
at the head of the stairs to cheer us through, cues raised on

high, and we had to walk that gauntlet to reach the even more rickety stairs that led to the private pool precinct above. Some quite rude remarks were heard amid what was a general raspberry, as our brave brigade made its way aloft. Play commenced, above and below, and the best that can be said for the arrangement is that it was a modest success.

It was not that the tables were not good — they were better than anything our side had ever played upon. But those Bronx cheers had done it, and the experiment lasted only one season before fading.

By the time the new Club premises were opened with Mr Justice Jerome's bequest of three tables, most of the Club's brigade of players had either dispersed or had lost interest or were deceased. Even as this is being written, efforts are being made to revive interest among the membership, failing which there is the threat that the billiard room will be turned into a revenue-producing place for power lunches, breakfasts, dinners and drinks.

Should that happen, we ask, would the startling Morrisseau print survive?

The Dear Old Place

he corner of Wellington
and Metcalfe streets where the old Club stood is like the
gap of a lost tooth in the face of Parliament.

The powers-that-be have tried to gussy it up with trees
and benches, flags and posters. The chip wagons line up at
the curb below where the Club's reading room used to be.
The smell of frying fat drifts into the windows of the Prime
Minister's office in the Langevin Block across the street.

Even while older members admit that things are better
now, the memories that vacant corner evokes in them will
remain as long as their dwindling ranks keep the old
emotions alive, boring the younger members with their
tales of the Good Old Days, and the Dear Old Club.

But, we are asked, wasn't the food crummy?

Yes it was, though it was always nicely served, and it
was cheap.

And wasn't the place musty?

Shabby was the word. Paint flaking, carpets worn
through in places. Heating system on its last legs, radiators
rattling. Turn-of-the-century wiring with ancient switches
and plugs. Uncomfortable furniture throughout. The top
floor derelict and closed off, and that magnificent central

staircase denounced by the fire marshal as a funnel for the flames. Brass chandeliers tarnished to the point of blackness, and the gold leaf ceiling of the Dining Room dulled into tawdriness.

"Sombre" was the word Peter C. Newman used to describe clubland in his 1975 book, *The Canadian Establishment*. He called it "the heavy hush of privilege", and he quoted Cleveland Amory on the club ethic: "It is here and only here the member can find his four freedoms: freedom of speech against democracy; freedom of worship of aristocracy; freedom from want of tipping; and above all, freedom from fear of women."

Newman quoted a Club habitué as saying that "belonging to clubs takes the guesswork out of friendships", and he listed the Rideau Club as a national institution that really counted, along with the York, Toronto, and National clubs in Toronto, the Mount Royal and St James's in Montreal, and the Vancouver Club.

Of the Rideau, Newman said it had "a distinctive air missing from some of its lesser cousin institutions."

So it had.

It also had that best pool room in the country, six tables well used every lunchtime, and sometimes into the evenings, while poker games raged into the night in smaller rooms.

Above all there was the balcony, facing the Hill, giving Club members the greatest front-row seats in

Canada for national spectacles. It was from there that we saw Prime Minister Lester Pearson, later to be Club President, light the Centennial Flame on the New Year's Eve that ushered in 1967. From there we watched Dominion Day grow into a theatrical spectacular, and events like royal visitations, the first flying of the Maple Leaf Flag, and the mounting tide of protest demonstrations that made the Hill seem a site of perpetual strife.

Part of the advance on the government's expropriation money was used, after 1972, to plan renovations. There was even consideration of a sprinkler system, though repeated inspections concluded that nothing could prevent the old place going up like a tinderbox if it ever caught fire.

In 1977, tenders were called for redecoration. Simpsons department store put in a proposal that some members deemed too splashy, too much gilt, and just plain not very good. But out went the old rugs, the old chandeliers, the old furniture, all sold at auction, and all treasured now by those who lugged the stuff away, especially the chandeliers which, when cleaned and polished, became collector's items in houses from Halifax to Vancouver.

And in went new fixtures, new plumbing, new wiring, new beams to hold the place up. New professional management promised better and brighter things, especially when the Club hired master chef Christian Hitz from the Chateau Champlain in Montreal and made him part of the team headed by the new Manager, Al Hofer.

The newly decorated clubhouse was our pride and joy. We were just getting a taste for the new menus and the presence of women in our midst, giving a new dimension to that old Club word, fellowship. In the past, fathers and sons had enjoyed a Club tradition of Christmas Eve jug-up lunches together, while mothers and daughters lunched below stairs in their own compound. Now this developed into an all-family Christmas Eve tradition in the main lounge, knocking a lot of the stuffiness out of the premises. The Club was still a place where almost everybody knew almost everybody else, or wanted to.

We thought we were set for another ten years in the clubhouse, and there was even talk of putting in squash courts and other attractions for the younger set, who continued to shun the place. But then the grand staircase fulfilled the fire marshal's prophecy, and with a mighty roar the place burned to the ground.

Everything gone. Even the ghosts.

Real ghosts, they were, sworn to in the dead of night by people who heard them and smelled the smoke of their cigars in the old card room where, when nobody was playing, the clatter of the poker chips and the shuffling of the cards still echoed down the stairs. The phantom poker players gave the clubhouse its only air of romance, because men in clubhouses tend not to be a romantic lot.

Whose ghosts they were was never established, but their presence was not doubted, and it was assumed they adhered to the Club rules about limited bets, though they left no trace. The old clubhouse was definitely haunted, perhaps by old Sir John A. himself, though there was no smell of gin.

But there are others than ghosts residing in the memories and stories of the older members of the Club — such as the memorable Archie Lacelle, the hall porter and keeper of the keys who began working for the Club shortly after the turn of the century and remained for more than 55 years, most of them as guardian of the gate.

Any stranger who tried to pass him and ascend the stairs in the old clubhouse would get a curt "Who are you and where are you going?"

If the intruder was an invited guest, he would be shown to the Strangers' Room to await his host, who would be summoned from above by Archie.

Once, a cabinet minister who had been nominated for membership brought two guests for lunch, only to be told by Archie that the votes had not yet been counted and that he should take his party to the Chateau Laurier down the street. When the membership was subsequently confirmed, Archie was heard to snort: "If I'd had a vote he'd never have got in — I'd have deposited enough no's to make sure of that!"

When Archie retired in 1961, a fund for him subscribed by members amounted to $1911.50, from which was deducted the cost of a lazy boy chair, $205.00, and an inscribed silver tray costing $134.00, leaving a balance of $1,572.50. It was decided to supplement this by a transfer from the staff Christmas fund sufficient to bring the amount to $1,700. Archie died in 1964 and rated a reverent chapter in the 1965 Club history, ending with "Requiescat in pace."

Through most of its long life, the Rideau Club was regarded as a symbol of the WASP establishment in Canada. For at least half of those years it functioned as an outpost of Empire, its moods and modes derived from its London models, with variations.

At first glance it might seem odd that today's revived and revised Rideau Club is operated by people who are mostly Swiss and German. But as Swiss-born General Manager Alfons Hofer puts it, "Who else knows the business?" And as a business, serious money is involved — from the substantial entrance fee to the fine, pricey wine list and the best service in town.

Mr Hofer is a native of Zurich who had a distinguished career in Swiss and Belgian hotels before emigrating to Canada in 1952. He became maitre d' of Ottawa's memorable La Touraine restaurant in the Roxborough apartment hotel. That building was owned by Russell Blackburn, a long-time member of the Rideau Club but no admirer of its food. He described La Touraine as a place where he could take his friends for a decent meal. Mr Hofer was wooed away from La Touraine to come on strength at the Rideau Club in 1979, just before the fire. He shepherded the Club through the interim years and has been a prime factor in its present success.

Senior Hostess Maria Lengemann is a native of Germany who has been with the Rideau Club for 27 years and regards the Club as her life. Members would put it the other way around.

Chef Peter Adeelberg is German, as is Assistant Chef Gunther Sankowski. Night Chef Werner Lederman is Swiss.

And the conscience of the Club, usually found at his desk in the reception area, is Rupert Westmaas, a native of Guyana.

Hostess Joan O'Neill, who is in charge of the Club in the evening hours, is from Cape Breton.

So the only native Ottawan on the senior staff is Administrator Doris Curran, who has been with the Club since 1945.

There was a time when the Club Manager was also a full member. The idea was that he would thus be able to talk to the members man-to-man, but this did not always work exactly as hoped.

One day a member, known for his habit of always wearing white gloves, stormed into the office of the member-Manager, Mr Fairweather, and showed his gloves, blackened on the palms.

"Got that from the bannisters," he complained. "The man who's supposed to dust them isn't on the job!"

"Well then," was the Manager's reply, "we can get rid of him and save the money. All we have to do is have you run your gloves over them every morning!"

The Club had a number of characters in those days, members notable for their personality quirks. One of these was Mr Biggar, who was notorious for admonishing his fellow members for conduct he found unseemly, or not in accord with Club regulations.

One day Mr Biggar dressed down a veteran member for some minor transgression, and read him the riot act within the hearing of others in the lounge. The offending member spoke with a trace of English accent, as was not uncommon in those days, and when Mr Biggar was out of earshot, was heard to say: "Gad! Have you evah known a biggah buggah than that buggah Biggah?"

There is much now to mourn — old friends, old times, old traditions, old ties, old comrades. And, most of all, an old building.

It may seem odd to put a building at the top of a pile of emotions, above people and things loved and lost. But it was possible to love that old place, and not just in the way one might love an old coat, or an old pair of shoes, or an old car. The old clubhouse was, in truth, greater than the sum of its parts or its people.

It helped if you cared about this country, this town, this Parliament and all the things to which the old white clubhouse bore testimony — the policies hatched, the fishing trips planned, the talkative noons and the festive nights, the billiard games with beady-eyed young hustlers, or with misty-eyed shooters like Gordon Gale, still winning in his nineties, and Judge Hyndman, having a good day with his cue in his eighties, or threatening to sell it when his shots were off.

Kindly anglers would distribute fishing flies for the trout and salmon seasons — Tec Morphy had his own patterns for the Magannassippi Club lakes; Shirley Woods designed a green salmon fly for Quebec's Old Fort River and named it "Roger's Fancy", for the fishing companion who inspired it and caught the first salmon on it, Major General Roger Rowley.

After the clubhouse was destroyed, it became the fashion not to lament its loss. This very book testifies that it was, in fact, a blessing. But in talking about the old Club's shortcomings to a fellow member just the other day, I joined in when he threw his head back and gave a great laugh, saying: "But God, it was a grand old place!"

Yes, it was.

Bytown Revisited

*T*he warm editorial quoted earlier from the *Ottawa Journal* was written by I. Norman Smith, one of the journalist members of the Rideau Club, like his father before him. As previously noted, the Club has always had a fair smattering of media members, usually to the unease of the rest, concerned about their privacy. There have been outbursts of indignation about irreverent treatment of the Club in the public prints, but no horse-whipping, no expulsions.

Norman Smith was that rarity among journalists, a genuine gentleman, respected both in the Bohemia of print and in the best of circles. Of the Club he loved, he wrote: "The place was devoted to the proposition, London in origin, that a day's work is made not only bearable but even desirable, provided a man can mix good talk with good food at midday."

Had he lived, Norman perhaps would have written the story of the Rideau Club, though at one time he suggested me for the job, putting aside his misgivings about a barbarian newshound at the gate eager to divulge things best kept behind closed doors.

I am indebted to him for many treasured memories, not only of the Club but of Ottawa, the history of which he had researched on the Club's behalf as part of the tapestry of which the Club was a part.

In the paragraphs that follow I have borrowed extensively from Norman's informal history of the Club, contained in a speech he gave at the Club's Anniversary Dinner on February 8, 1978. I have used some of Norman's exact words, interwoven with my own, to give a taste of his account.

If Sir Wilfrid Laurier could see us now he would not be surprised at the way the twentieth century has belonged to Canada. After all, it's what he predicted for his country, and most of it has happened in terms of wealth, health and happiness, though he might not have foreseen the extent to which Canada would become a land of city dwellers with the treasured rural way of life giving way to the frantic urban.

And if that would surprise Sir Wilfrid, picture his astonishment at what the century has done for the nation's capital, a place of which he and so many others once despaired. To see it now, its avenues and waterways projecting the best of the twentieth century, poised to leap into the twenty-first, is to view one of the fairest cities and finest capitals in the world.

It remains a government town but tourism is its second industry and Parliament Hill ranks in the list of

global "sights" to see. Business thrives and mills give way
not only to ultra-modern museums but to high-technology
industries that rim the ever-expanding periphery of the city
and its satellites. The fastest-growing cities in Quebec are
across the river from Ottawa and some of the most spectacular federal buildings are located there, with more
in progress.

The three great hinterlands, north along the
Gatineau, east and west along the Ottawa and south-west
along the Rideau River, are unrivalled in the world for
variety, recreation and outdoor sports, all within drives
that are reckoned in minutes, not hours. And amid all
this, the cultural and social life of the city thrives, for
young and old alike.

Dwellers in other cities might claim similar blessings
while resenting that so many of their tax dollars are spent
to glorify Ottawa. But while residents of the capital get
most of the day-to-day benefits, visitors increasingly take
pride in what they find, reacting more and more the way
Americans do when they visit Washington, D.C.

The most remarkable thing about Ottawa is that, in
the short space of 30 years, it has passed from being a
largely English-speaking village into a bilingual metropolis,
a place where French is heard in public places as much
as English.

And yet for all its grand public buildings and
highrises, it is a place where the new melds into the old

and where the oldest man-made relic, the Rideau Canal, has been made into one of the recreational, all-season wonders of the modern world.

Romance abounds, from the 1613 footprints of Samuel de Champlain portaging on what he hoped was his way to China, to the 1826 arrival of Colonel John By, intent on sinking a million pounds of British money into a waterway out of range of American guns. He called the place Bytown, a name that proved less durable than his works, which in places rival the pyramids of ancient Egypt, and promise to last as long or at least leave as long a trace, come ice and high water.

By 1854, Bytown had a population of 9,000 and was incorporated as the City of Ottawa, after the Ootaooa branch of the Algonquin Indians to whom the name meant "large ears". Spell it any way you like — in French it's Outaouais, as hard for the English to pronounce as Ottawa is for the French. In the light of subsequent history, the Indian word for "big mouth" might have been more suitable for the seat of government.

That it would be the seat was not settled until 1857, after Kingston, Montreal, Toronto and Quebec City had been tried as capitals of the United Province of Canada. But the French didn't want Toronto, the English didn't want Quebec, and Montreal lost its claim when the citizens burned the Legislature in 1849. Kingston came close, but was too near the Yankee menace.

So Queen Victoria was asked "that Your Majesty
will be graciously pleased to exercise your Royal preroga-
tive and select some one place for the permanent seat of
Government in Canada."

By December of 1857, the Queen ruled, to the astonishment and dismay of just about all concerned, that
"Ottawa is selected." Ten years later, the British North
America Act declared that Ottawa would be the seat of
government "until the Queen desires otherwise." By that
time, the buildings were up on Barracks Hill, re-named
Parliament Hill or just the Hill, destined to be the most
imposing television backdrop in the country, a hundred
years on.

Stephen Leacock once mused that the capital had
the merit of such scenic beauty and solitude that no enemy
could find it.

Laurier in 1884 said, "I would not wish to say anything disparaging of the capital but it is hard to say anything good of it. Ottawa is not a handsome city and does
not appear to be destined to become one."

Liberal leader George Brown said the Parliament
Buildings were 500 years ahead of their time and that to
light, heat and keep them clean would cost half the revenue of the United Province. Some hundred years later,
a project to build a fourth building on the block that
included the Rideau Club, to finish the Parliamentary
precinct, was dropped when it was found that it would cost

as much a year to heat and clean as the original Centre Block had cost to build.

Young Mackenzie King, arriving in Ottawa in 1900, said "the business part of the town is small and like that of a provincial town, not interesting but tiresome." King himself was tiresome but the physical works he inspired did more to make Ottawa interesting than anything done by others.

Goldwin Smith, philosopher and snob, found Ottawa "a sub-Arctic lumber village converted by royal mandate into a political cockpit."

Criticisms have abounded through the years, the most usual comparison being with the Outer Mongolian capital of Ulan Bator.

The year Sir John A. and his fellow "Fathers of Confederation" formed the Rideau Club was 1865 and the population of Ottawa was 18,000, depending on how many were in from the woods.

The City Directory of the time noted that many wagon drivers were French Canadians who were "not over-scrupulous as to their non-religious sentiments expressed to parties standing in the way, or to their own hard-worked animals." These tendencies can be found in the unclerical lingo of the Outaouais to this day, where sacrilegious cursing reaches a pinnacle of eloquence.

Streets were mud, sidewalks were single planks, and
Parliament was best approached from Government House
by boat.

There was one daily newspaper and four breweries, as
against today's three dailies and no breweries of consequence in the city that spawned Carlings, Bradings,
O'Keefe's and that one-time magnate of suds, E.P. Taylor.

The *Citizen* failed to record the birth of the Rideau
Club on September 18, but it did carry this item: "Police
Court: Alderman [R.W.] Scott presiding. Mary Roach,
vagrancy; fined $5, or 21 days in gaol. Mary chose the
latter alternative." Alderman Scott became Mayor Scott,
Senator Scott, Sir Richard Scott, and the grandfather of
Cuthbert Scott who, as President of the Rideau Club, was
the target of feminist wrath during the last stage of male
supremacy inside the portals. And Cuthbert was the father
of one of the Club's most recent Presidents, David Scott,
under whose regime this book was commissioned.

Davidson's, the Montreal Chemists, were offering "a
perfect substitute for spirituous liquors for those wishing to
escape from the degrading slavery of intemperance."

Her Majesty's Theatre, standing where the National
Press Building is now on Wellington Street, was playing
"Paul Pry, or I Hope I Don't Intrude", to full houses of
1,000 people.

St Mary's Academy for Young Ladies, run by the Grey
Sisters, was advertising a course of education that "will

embrace all the useful and ornamental branches and the strictest attention will be paid to the moral and polite deportment of the pupils. Tuition per annum $16, extras per annum for piano $30, and for Drawing and Painting $10."

Gas street lights were, by law, to be lighted "only in the dull period of the moon."

Steamers on the Rideau Canal ran twice a week to Kingston, leaving at 7 a.m. and arriving at 11 a.m. next day.

In the four provinces that comprised the new Dominion there were just over three million people and Montreal, at 107,000, was twice as big as Toronto. New Brunswick wanted out of Confederation the year after joining and Prince Edward Island didn't want to join at all. Leacock wrote: "[O]f the nineteen members from Nova Scotia all except Dr Charles Tupper went to Ottawa only to protest against being there."

In 1867, there were 280 civil servants in Ottawa, and the big business in town was lumber, not government. At what was then Head Office in Westminster, fewer than 500 officials and aides were running the entire British Empire, at a time when it was an enterprise on which the sun never set. Parkinson's Law had not yet emerged, but its principles were in place. In 1868, yearly Dominion government receipts were $18,000,000, payments were $17,000,000. Today, for Parliament alone, the Senate costs $34,000,000, the Commons $200,000,000, and the Library $15,000,000, per year.

In 1868, Members of Parliament shared offices during the two-month sessions and their travel allowance was 10 cents a mile. Annual pay and expenses totalled under $1,000. There were no secretaries on the Hill until a pool with 50 employees was set up in 1916. Now, more than 2,000 people work on the Hill and they generate 50,000,000 pieces of mail a year, handled by 51 postal workers. Note that in 1885 the entire national post office had 56 workers, making it the biggest department in government. A newspaper of the time, lamenting the slow postal service, wrote: "Why such a state of things should still exist is hard to explain."

The early civil servants had to do military duty under penalty of dismissal, drilling twice a week on Parliament Hill where today's "chocolate soldiers" change the guard for tourists. They carried muzzle loaders and live ammunition.

It was in this setting that the Rideau Club was founded, "for social purposes," it not being deemed necessary to stipulate that it would be a gentleman's club, there being no other kind.

The petition of Hon. John A. Macdonald was received and read in the Legislative Assembly at Quebec on August 25, 1865, during the fourth session of the eighth parliament.

The private bill was given the fast track to beat the closing of the session: it received second reading on September 8, passed through committee in a day, was passed by the Assembly on the 14th, given Legislative Council approval on the 18th, followed by immediate royal assent by Lord Monck, who signed by his own hand just before terminating the session and moving the seat of government to Ottawa, preparatory to Confederation two years later.

For all its high-sounding beginnings, the Club immediately ran into problems that were to trouble its members right into present times — drinking, insolvency and non-payment of house accounts by members who, in the words of one chronicler, "deemed it ungentlemanly to pay their bills."

Rules of behaviour decreed that three subjects were not to be discussed on the premises — women, religion and politics. There were 85 ordinary members and 23 privileged; the entrance fee was $80 and annual dues $20. Bets were not to exceed one dollar and only Whist, Ecarte, Piquet and Pool were to be played for money, plus one dice game, Backgammon. By 1887 the price of a dinner was 60 cents, dessert extra; in 1868 a bottle of Chablis cost 60 cents, with Chateau Lafitte at $1.35, a special price for members of the executive committee, headed by John A.

For a monthly wage of $30, the cook was instructed to "be guided in her attendance by the requirements of the

Club, say, from 8:00 a.m. to 10:30 p.m. or later if necessary." Kitchen slops were sold to a Mrs Reynolds for $20 a year. It was not until 1917 that, as a war measure, it was decreed that women be allowed to serve at table.

For its first four years the Rideau Club was located at the southeast corner of Wellington and Kent streets, in the same building as Doran's Hotel and the Bank of Montreal.

In 1870, the Club moved to the Queen's Restaurant, on Wellington near Metcalfe, where the Langevin Block housing the Prime Minister's office now stands. In 1876, the Club built its first building on the site it would occupy for 103 years, facing, if not commanding, Parliament Hill.

It was not plain sailing, as witness the report of an emergency committee in 1868 on the Club's deficit:

> The heaviest items of . . . expenditure are, of course, servants' wages and provisions. Hitherto very nearly the same staff of servants has been kept up all the year round although, in point of fact, their services are seldom called into requisition except during the short period of the year in which the legislature is in session. Your Committee would, therefore, recommend that after the prorogation of Parliament this year, the present staff should be reduced to the Steward, his wife and a boy to attend as marker in the Billiard room and perform any other duties as yard or errand boy that may be required of him. . . .
>
> During the two previous sessions of Parliament, the number of Members frequenting the Club for breakfast, dinner, billiards, cards, etc. was sufficiently large to give on an average a profit of something like $1,420.00.
>
> In estimating the profits for this year the Committee have based their calculations upon a session of only six

weeks, but even should the session extend over a longer period it would depend entirely upon the support given to the Club by its Members, whether the present very moderate estimate can be realized.

Your Committee would therefore strongly urge upon those Members of the Club who are Members of Parliament, the absolute necessity which exists for making use of the Club as much as possible during their stay in Ottawa, as without the profits which the Club derives from their expenditure during the session, the annual income . . . would not be sufficient to meet the annual expenditure, and there would consequently be no other course left, than to close the establishment.

The Club auctioned its furniture to raise money in 1869, and rented out its billiard table, the annual meeting in 1871 attracting only five members.

That year, a committee was struck to consider whether to continue the Club as a year-round venture, or during Parliamentary session only, or to fold altogether. Cooler and more affluent heads prevailed, to the point where, by 1875, the Rideau Club Building Association was able to proceed with the new clubhouse on what was known as Notman Corner, a portion of the Sparks Estate, the vendors being the noted pioneer photographers, Mr and Mrs William J. Topley.

It was a site that was the glory of the Club for most of 100 years, eventually becoming a burden that was almost to put the Club out of business, only to turn out in the end to be the source of wealth, salvation, and today's prosperity.

In 1979, most members would have preferred the Club
to stay in the old premises facing Parliament, even though
most of the links with parliamentarians had been broken.
The United States Embassy, long contemplating a move
from the property next door to the Club, eventually aban-
doned the proposition and decided to stay put, there being
no more prestigious site in the city, even in the land.

For the Club, the forced move proved providential,
but it left memories that will last some members their
lifetimes, however short. Partly, it is pure sentiment,
happy memories of what seemed quieter and saner times.
Partly, it is a requiem for old institutions that were linked
by threads from the "mother country" — every city had a
club, and some have them still, either reborn or in the
mausoleum format. As one chronicler put it, "the
gentleman's club enjoyed a nineteenth century boom,
bastion of those 'sensible men of substantial means who are
what we wish to be ruled by'." English clubs melded the
professions and the aristocracy, building on relationships
established at the public schools. The Canadian pattern
may have been a pale imitation, but it was there; Canadian
high society may not be as caste-ridden as the British, but
it is there, too, the chief differences being that untitled old
money doesn't go back so far, and new money is not as
suspect, socially.

Nor are there the eccentricities the British do so well
— for instance, the first Duke of Westminster inviting a

horse to a garden party he gave on Park Lane to celebrate
Queen Victoria's Golden Jubilee.

One over-stimulated London clubman once shot out
all the street lights on Pall Mall and then worked his way
back along the street, pelting golf balls with his driver.
High spirits, the English called it, though had people of
lower station tried it, it would have been hooliganism.
Rideau Club members reserved such antics for their
fishing camps.

Card games have always been a part of club life in
Canada; at the Royal Ottawa the game is bridge, and at
the Rideau Club the tradition has been poker — poker
on Saturday afternoons and Monday nights, when players
could have the place to themselves, except for the
attendance of the faithful Cora to tend to the light
refreshments.

Most of the poker players are members of the Club,
but not all — privileged strangers are often invited to
round out the table of ten, and a lot of cigar chomping goes
on to this day, without fear of complaints from the finicky.

In times past, when poker was played every night,
often into the morning hours, the Club tried to limit the
stakes. Today, the Club turns a blind eye to what the
poker players bet and when you try to find out you are told
to let yourself be dealt in and you will know. All players
deny the old test that if you have to ask, you can't afford it.

And so far, no women have asked, though the

assumption is that they would be welcomed if they did, just as they can take a cue any time in the billiard room, but none ever has, at least in tournament play.

The ones who livened up the town and the Club in the early days were the lumber barons, plus the annual influx of politicians balancing the old school ties and the boys of the old brigade.

During the Second World War there was the flow of the dollar-a-year men to go with Big Government which, like the income tax of the First World War, was here to stay. With it came that new upper middle class, the public service mandarins, as identifiable as the new breed of pundits in the media. The senior civil servants endured in the Rideau Club even after successive Prime Ministers wanted the Club boycotted — and when they quit their high posts to join the growing legion of consultants, they led a van of new Club members, mostly men, but now including some women.

These, along with people from all of the professions, now form the main and most lucrative portion of the Club's patronage. In the posh premises atop the midtown office tower, they join the captains of business and industry, and their pathfinders and navigators — lawyers, accountants, lobbyists, public relations operatives and the "usual suspects" of clubland, the stockbrokers, bankers and underwriters.

The result is a Club that is not the way it was at all.

Dues and Don'ts

*M*ost of the records of the Rideau Club were destroyed in the 1979 fire, though a few charred leather-bound books survived to give some of the flavour of times gone by, without much of the sauce.

The Rideau Club history of 1965, written by Commander C.H. Little, preserves some amusing bits, including this 1939 proposal, later implemented, for bedrooms:

> There is abundance of space under the Club's roof for the provision of sleeping accommodation for members . . . [and] five bedrooms can be provided in the Southeast corner of the building on the Card Room floor at a cost which might be considered to justify the Club in incurring the expense involved.
>
> This scheme involves the use of the present Silence Room, a large Card Room to the South of it, the Poker Room and two small rooms next to the lavatory. The Silence Room and the Poker Room would serve as bedrooms without changes other than redecoration. . . . [A] proper rate of charge for the bedrooms would be about $2.00 a night, with provision for a monthly charge of about $45.00.

For many years, the bedrooms were rented to members on a long-term basis. Ultimately they were removed on orders of the fire marshal, with the House Committee concurring.

Two themes run through the Club record books that survived the fire: the reluctance of some members to pay their dues on time, and the tendency of members to filch newspapers and periodicals from the Club library. There were, and are, few books on the shelves worth pinching, but billiard cues and balls have to be locked away.

Records of other clubs in other cities reveal the same problems. This may indicate a greater hesitancy on the part of the well-to-do to pay their bills than of those of more modest means, or perhaps a haughty disdain for the vulgarity of the paying of accounts. It might also indicate that many people of modest means became members of the Rideau Club; certainly, there were many who came downtown by street car in other days, and many still travel by bus today, though this may have more to do with parking problems than with cash flow, since parking costs $10 a day.

The most agonizing problem faced by Club Managers, past and present, was the "posting" on the Club board of the names of delinquent members. As for tracking down members who filch papers and magazines from the library, no procedure has ever been found, there being no paper detection machines and strip searches having been ruled out. Members may sign up to buy old magazines and some of the latter actually are disposed of in this way.

A succession of hall porters have tried to police comings and goings, weeding out "strangers" or men who try to enter without proper dress, jacket and tie being required. Along with jackets, a supply of Club ties is kept on hand to avoid undue embarrassment, and these are properly severe in design: solid background of dark blue, with a tiny Club crest in gold, the tie itself being unfashionably long and wide.

Author Shirley Woods, in *Ottawa, The Capital of Canada*, tells the Rideau Club story this way:

> The Rideau Club, Ottawa's oldest and most prestigious men's club, was incorporated by an Act of Parliament on 18 September 1865. . . .
>
> The club has many long-standing traditions. One is that briefcases must be checked with the hall porter, and no business papers may be displayed in the public rooms. . . .
>
> In recent years the Rideau Club has been lampooned by the press as a stuffy bastion of the Establishment. In defence of the club, it should be pointed out that since its inception, the atmosphere has been as informal as one's home. Sir John A. Macdonald and his boon companion, the Honourable Thomas D'Arcy McGee had many song-filled evenings in the club's room at Doran's Hotel. One of their favourite ditties ended with the refrain:
>
> A drunken man is a terrible curse
>
> But a drunken woman is twice as worse. . . .
>
> Ottawa society was sharply stratified at the turn of the century. Membership in a gentleman's club was restricted to those who were well connected (by birth or by marriage) and those in certain favoured professions. So pronounced was the social pecking order that while medical doctors were usually welcomed, dentists were normally refused membership. Retail merchants and men engaged in trade — unless they were both educated and

wealthy — were excluded from the more prestigious clubs.

In 1904 this situation prompted three well-known members of the Rideau Club to establish a new entity, the Laurentian Club. These men, Edward R. Bremner, R. Gordon Edwards, and Colonel (later Sir) Percy Sherwood, took this action because they wanted a club where they could mingle with friends from all walks of life. That same year the three founders signed a bank loan for $10,000, which was used to buy modest premises on Slater Street. Colonel Sherwood, who at that time was commissioner of the Dominion Police Force, which had jurisdiction over the Parliament buildings, was the first president of the Laurentian Club.

By 1913, when the membership was approaching 200, the club moved to a newly erected building at the corner of Albert and Elgin streets. . . . Twenty years later the club was hit by the Depression, and the situation eventually deteriorated to the extent that it was unable to pay its taxes. The club managed to survive this ordeal, but in 1941 the federal government expropriated its building and this forced a move to 233 Metcalfe Street. . . .

The turning point came in 1947, when the executors of the C. Jackson Booth Estate sold Jackson Booth's former residence at 252 Metcalfe Street to the Laurentian Club. The sale, made for a token price, was executed with the understanding that the club would try to keep the house in its original state. Booth's turreted red brick mansion, which has eight fireplaces, large rooms, and ornate wood panelling, makes a fine club.

So, what was, and is, so special about the Rideau Club?

Every city has a club. Some cities have several, each of them regarded by its members as "the" club in town. All of them have had crises — social, racial, financial, political — just as the Rideau Club has had. Clubdom is in trouble everywhere, nowhere more so than in the British capital that started it all, where assorted manipulations and amalgamations have been necessary to keep the most legendary of clubs alive as something more than hangovers from the nineteenth century on the eve of the twenty-first.

But of the one-time gentlemen's clubs, only the Rideau Club has involved so many Prime Ministers and Governors General in its ups and downs, suffering in the process various boycotts and blackballs, while instigating not a few of its own. What other club could boast incorporation by act of a fledgling parliament that met in Quebec City, two years before the capital of the new nation was established in Ottawa?

The names of the founders are inscribed in that act of the Legislative Council and Assembly of Canada, precursors of the Senate and the House of Commons: John A. Macdonald, George Etienne Cartier, George Brown, John Carling, A.T. Galt, Hector L. Langevin, J.J.C. Abbott, Thomas D'Arcy McGee, Alonzo Wright, J.M. Currier, Allan Gilmour, C.S. Gzowski, to name a few.

The Club minutes casually introduce the names of the famous.

From 1868:

The Hon. Mr McGee having denied, by telegram, all indebtedness to the Club it was ordered that, on his return to Ottawa, a detailed statement of such indebtedness be furnished to him. [He attended the annual meeting on March 31, 1877.]

And this on June 5, 1889:

A complaint was made by Mr Sandford Fleming that he was overcharged for wines served at two lunches. Mr Fleming paid the account but stated that he did so feeling confident that more wines were charged to him than were consumed by his guests. The Secretary informed the Steward that the Committee were perfectly satisfied with his statements and accounts rendered to Mr Fleming.

And much later, this, in 1964:

Mr P. Michael Pitfield wrote a letter suggesting that additional kinds of better cheese should be served in the dining room. The Committee decided that with fourteen brands of cheese from six different countries served from the cheese wagon the variety was adequate.

"Under ordinary conditions," says a Club bulletin of 1915, "it would have been natural to have marked the semi-centennial of the Club by some gathering of the members. But it was decided, after much consultation, that however much we might desire to take note of such an anniversary, circumstances prevailed against any general celebration at the time."

Ah, you might think, they were observing the darkest days of the Great War, out of reverence for the fallen, whose names were listed on the Club's Roll of Honour.

But no. The fact was, the Rideau Club was broke — not for the first time in its life and certainly not for the last. The cost of pre-war construction of the lavish new club premises, across the street from Parliament Hill, had gone way over the estimates of the time and resulted in "a somewhat unfortunate financial position."

"Receipts from entrance fees," the bulletin went on, "almost immediately after construction and from that time on have fallen below expectations. Apart from these troubles, but to a degree consequent upon them, the ordinary operations of the Club have not resulted profitably so that repeated deficits occurred."

So, no semi-centennial party — the Club was house-poor, and that blessed building, new, middle-aged or old, would remain a burden until the day it burned to the ground and cascaded a jackpot into the Club's coffers, making possible celebrations on today's scale. But the Club had frequent money troubles even before it owned a building, as the following selections from the Club minutes reveal.

1867:
The Committee regret to be under the necessity of adverting here to the difficulty they have experienced during the past year in the collection from members of their annual subscriptions, some of which, for 1867, are still unpaid. The efforts of the Committee to promote the well being of the Club have been greatly retarded by this slowness.

May 16, 1868:
The Chairman stated that he considered it better that the Club should be maintained purely as a Parliamentary Club, closing it during Recess with the exception of the

servants necessary to preserve the furniture, and that he feared, otherwise, the Club could not be carried on with satisfactory results financially. It was suggested that a proper measure, under present circumstances, would be to remove the Club, if possible, to the building in the Parliament grounds, lately used as offices for the Board of Public Works, that by doing so the Club would be more accessible to Members, and that therefore much of the business which is now absorbed by the restaurants in the Houses of Parliament would be done in the Club House.

October 23, 1868:

Members of the Executive Committee may, in future, have wines at the undermentioned prices: Moselle, .60; Pontet Canet, $1.00; St. Estephe, .70; Chablis, .60; Vouvray, .80; Bordeaux, .40; Burgundy, .80; Champagne, $1.35; Hungarian, $1.10; Hock, $1.80; Chateau Palmer & Chateau Lafitte, $1.35. Meals of Executive Committee at each weekly meeting be considered part of the ordinary expenses of the Club, to be borne by it, and to be charged to expense account.

Mr Cassels brought before the Committee the necessity for providing for consumption in the Club wines of a better quality than those at present obtainable, and that the wines now in stock are generally of an inferior quality.

March 11, 1869:

Mr White strongly deprecated the idea of closing the Club, pointing out the necessity which existed in the requirements of parliamentary members for such an establishment and the difficulty which would exist in commencing another club were the present one allowed to become extinct.

March 12, 1869, Secretary to MPs:

I am desired by the Executive Committee to express the hope that in view of the great necessity which exists for securing to the Club a greater amount of support than it has hitherto received, you will endeavour, as far as you possibly can, to promote the interests of the Club in such arrangements as you may make.

December 13, 1871:

The Secretary was further instructed to write specially to members more than one year in arrears for subscriptions, stating that . . . unless overdue subscriptions are paid in, the Executive Committee will be compelled to take legal steps for the collection of such subscriptions.

March 4, 1874:

All debts paid, Club solvent, thanks to E.P. Jones, Chief Steward. Ordinary members number 91, privileged 66, total 157. Receipts $6,060.25, expenditure $4,407.20.

A mood of optimism then took hold.

March 10, 1875:

Moved by Alonzo Wright, that the Executive Committee be empowered to purchase a suitable lot and make the necessary arrangements for the erection of a new Club House.

March 14, 1876:

A number of gentlemen formed themselves into an Association under the title of "The Club Building Association" and purchased "Notman Corner", so called with a view to the erection of the building now occupied by the Club. . . .

The furniture, carpets, etc. of the Club have all been purchased at the best possible advantage. . . .

Your Committee . . . beg to congratulate the Members of the Club on this occupancy of so eligible and commodious a Club House.

Eligible and commodious in 1876, but apparently insufficiently attractive to some potential members nine decades later.

1968:

It was pointed out that very few members of the present cabinet are members of the Club. It was agreed that the Membership Committee would approach members of the cabinet who are members of the Club to try and encourage more cabinet ministers, senators and senior civil servants to join the Rideau Club.

1969:

Correction in minutes: "Paragraph referring to the pressing need for a replacement for the dishwasher, matter passed to House Committee for study." This should read: "The House Committee was requested to investigate the possibility of purchasing a good used dishwasher and if none was available to purchase a new one." Dishwasher ordered at cost of $6,000.

1970:

Special assessment $30; annual subscription $275 ordinary, $335 privileged, $50 supernumerary. . . .

Attendance at Club dinner in honour of Chief Justice J.R. Cartwright was lower than anticipated and as a result we were barely able to meet expenses. . . .

A pressing need for new members, particularly among the younger generation, "young professional gentlemen getting established". . . .

One-hour free parking discontinued because it costs Club $60 a month, and "there has not been a sufficient increase in attendance to warrant the additional expense". . . .

Consideration should be given to extending the privileges of the Ladies Section to desirable Ladies of the community who are not wives or widows of members.

1973:

Since most of the diplomats arriving in Ottawa usually make themselves known to one of the local banks, it was suggested that the bank managers be canvassed to assist

the Membership Committee in their drive for new
privileged members.

December 13, 1973:

The board of directors were not in favour of approaching
the government to request that the Rideau Club be
declared an historical site.

President Pearson

*T*he founders called it
"a Club for social purposes", empowered to build a Club
House in the city of Ottawa, then a rough lumber town of
18,000 roistering souls, a town whose muddy streets were
rutted by the wheels of groaning horses and wagons, haul-
ing the stones and timbers for the new Parliament Buildings, rising by Queen Victoria's decree.

Legislators from across the land would find the new
capital a drab place indeed, but the Rideau Club could be
both a home-away-from-home and a refuge from the
battles of the day. The accent would be on smoking,
drinking, eating and gaming, and one of the biggest jokes
about the Club was to be the way members ignored the ban
on discussion of politics, religion and women. Not that
religion was much talked about, and women were scarcely
mentioned from one decade to the next. But political talk
echoed through the halls and chambers, and for a time in
this century the country was run from the Rideau Club
table that was the base of operations for Prime Minister
Richard Bedford Bennett.

Prime Minister Bennett was a regular for lunch until, as R.A.J. Phillips says in his *Reader's Digest* article,

> H.H. Stevens, his Minister of Trade and Commerce, in a violent parting of the ways, resigned to form the Reconstruction Party. Stevens made a practice of sitting ostentatiously in the lounge at the head of the stairs where his Prime Minister would be obliged to pass him. Rather than greet the rebel, Bennett took to lunching in his suite at the Chateau Laurier.

Membership in the Club came to be a sign of social rank in the capital and a blackball at the Club a social stigma. Snobs and nobs came to dominate the declining membership to the point where they almost drew the Club down into oblivion with them as class barriers dissolved.

Fishing and golf provided cross-bonds among the members — the Magannassippi, an overnight train ride away up the Ottawa River, where members once went to Spring Camp in their own private sleeping cars; The Five Lakes Fishing, where mandarins took their ease and launched plots that would be hatched at the Rideau Club; the Royal Ottawa and its Quebec neighbour, the Country Club, where nobody dreamed that business could be done in any language other than English.

Old money, old politics looked down their noses at new. And as social issues came to the fore in politics the elected representatives of the people, whose forebears had founded the Rideau Club, began to drift away. The only New Democrat ever to achieve (or, at least, accept) membership was Governor General Edward Schreyer and he did not deign to patronize the place. Oh, yes, and there was Graham Spry, that conscience of the CCF-NDP, one of the rare Canadians to be both an enthusiastic club man and a fervent socialist.

When Old Boys ran the land, the Rideau Club was network headquarters.

Gordon Robertson was the country's top public servant from 1963 to 1975, and he continued to patronize the Rideau Club even when John Diefenbaker, Joe Clark and Pierre Trudeau were shunning it and urging their colleagues to do the same.

In Robertson's words, a man's club is his club, and he enjoyed the Rideau Club. What is more, he used it in his own and his country's work — it was well known in the top echelon of bureaucrats and mandarins that during those years an invitation from Robertson to lunch at the Rideau Club often boded either good news or ill, and you never knew which until the cheese tray was brought around.

It was in this setting that senior public servants were sometimes told about their promotions, or lack of them, and deputy ministers and other senior officials went over problems, prospects and possible transfers from one department to another.

Sometimes a promotion entailed what for most of a century was the top mark of career achievement in the public service: membership in the Rideau Club itself.

The mandarinate continued to use the Rideau Club long after the politicians ceased to do so, and to this day there are more senior public servants in the Club for lunch, dinner and power seminars than there are cabinet ministers.

As for Robertson, he continues to be an enthusiastic member of the Club, and while he doesn't influence careers any more, he does his best to influence issues, including, recently, arguments with his old boss, Pierre Trudeau, over Meech Lake.

Robertson calls what he used to do "the senior personnel thing" and says he preferred to use the Rideau Club because "it's a nice place to talk privately about public matters."

The one Prime Minister who agreed with Robertson's assessment of the Rideau Club was Lester Pearson. Pearson is my nominee for Canadian of the Century, based more on his accomplishments in diplomacy than in domestic politics, though many think his political achievements as Prime Minister were more dramatic, with more lasting effect.

With Pearson, there was always the element of surprise, as with the Maple Leaf Flag, or changes in unemployment insurance to convert it into an income-redistribution scheme, or recognition that the English/French relationship was in a state of crisis. Collective bargaining in the public service, unification of the armed forces, medicare,

Canada Pension Plan — for a Prime Minister who never had a majority, he left a large mark on Canadian society, to match his Nobel Prize for saving the peace when global war threatened in 1956.

Pearson's preferred place for rest, recreation and a measure of business was not the East Block of Parliament, not the Centre Block, but the Rideau Club. It was here he had his conversations with colleagues; it was here he entertained distinguished statesmen of the world; and it was to the Rideau Club that he devoted considerable time and trouble, as its President, in the last year of his life.

One of Pearson's long-time colleagues, Escott Reid, tells in his memoirs (*Radical Mandarin*) of writing to Pearson, urging him to write his life's story.

"There will be many people," Reid told Pearson, "who will want to use you during your retirement for one cause or another — some good causes, some indifferent, some very good, but I plead with you not to allow your energies to be diverted from your main task."

Instead, Reid laments, Pearson did allow his energies to be diverted: "He undertook tasks, some of great importance, some of none." At the end of the list of diversions Pearson permitted himself, Reid notes: "He became president of the Rideau Club. The great memoirs he should have written were not written."

Pearson clearly did not deem the presidency of the Rideau Club to be an indifferent cause. He attended every meeting of the board during his presidency until, late in 1972, there is the poignant note that he was unable to attend due to illness, plus his assurance he would soon be back at the job. Within two months he was dead.

Pearson's affection for the Rideau Club reflected his feeling for Ottawa. Of all this century's Prime Ministers, only he and Mackenzie King really regarded the capital as home. Perhaps Sir Robert Borden's name might be added to this short list. Though his ties with Halifax remained strong, Borden, like King and Pearson, stayed in Ottawa after retirement. And, like Pearson, he served a term as President of the Rideau Club.

Mike Pearson never did make clear what impelled him to take the demanding job of Club President, though it may have been a desire to give back something of what the Club had given him throughout his years in diplomacy and politics. His feeling for the Club's value would go back to John A. Macdonald's reasons for founding the Club in the first place: to create a place where politicians, industrialists, business leaders and artists could meet in a congenial setting.

The ministers who served under Mackenzie King and Louis St Laurent were the last to use the Club extensively, and indeed to transact a good deal of the nation's business from there. Pearson was a member of both those governments and, during Mackenzie King's time, he had joined other mandarins and ministers at the Club, which served as a haven from the all-seeing eyes of King himself.

"I can still see those eyes boring into me and hear that voice," Pearson said as Prime Minister, long after King was dead. King had been active in the affairs of the Rideau Club in his earlier Ottawa years, but during his time as Prime Minister he left the premises to his ministers, content to drop in only occasionally and then to summon the required colleague into consultation at the foot of the grand staircase in the Strangers' Room.

It was in those times that John Diefenbaker came to regard the Rideau Club as a nest of Grits, and Pearson, first as Under Secretary and then as Secretary of State for External Affairs, was an obvious denizen. During the Diefenbaker boycott of the Club, Pearson, as Opposition Leader, continued his attendance, and as Prime Minister he encouraged use of the Club by his ministers and mandarins.

His assumption of the presidency, four years after his retirement from politics, put him at odds with the boycott of the Club encouraged by his successor, Pierre Elliott Trudeau. Indeed, it may have been the Trudeau boycott that moved Pearson to take an active hand in the Club's affairs, even though at the time no solution was in sight for the mounting problem of full membership for women. Maryon Pearson had been an early supporter of the feminist movement and, despite her coolness towards Trudeau, she was more likely to side with him than with her husband on the issue of women in the Rideau Club. In any event, she had never shared Pearson's enthusiasm for the Club and she could hardly have encouraged him to accept the presidency, though she did say "I married him for better or worse, but not for lunch."

Accept it he did, perhaps feeling that the Club needed him more than he needed the Club, given its declining fortunes and waning membership.

But his memoirs did suffer. As Escott Reid lamented, the Pearson memoirs faltered after the first two volumes, and had to be finished by committee, with disappointing results.

As for the Rideau Club, his rescue effort, if that was what he intended, failed despite the energies he brought to the task of Club President, traditionally the most thankless post in clubdom — and the most trouble-laden.

Certainly, he didn't undertake the office for the glory of the thing — club people are notoriously ungrateful to their executives, especially presidents. And club members tend not to notice honours accruing to their fellows, even those in service to their country. One who went to war for four years and came home festooned with decorations received this greeting: "Oh — been away?"

The Club records do contain this cryptic note, dated May 27, 1971: "Club President Lester B. Pearson has been awarded one of Britain's highest honours, the Order of Merit." But the minutes quickly get back to business.

As President, Pearson's attention to the everyday details of Club life was remarkable, as the following excerpts show — his signature is on minutes from matters as trivial as menus to the larger question of how to check the Club's decline by enticing younger men to join and even contemplating broader access for women.

1970:

The Committee noted that the service in the Main Lounge was not as good as the service in the top Lounge. It was suggested that the Girl at the small portable Bar stay at her Bar and one of the Girls serve the Members from that Bar.

The Secretary reported the inner curtains in the Ladies' Lounge were worn out and required replacement, cost $150. Secretary was authorized to purchase new curtains.

Henceforth the London *Times* and *New Statesman* are to come by airmail, but we hereby cancel *Blackwoods*, the *Calgary Herald, Canadian Historical Review, Dalhousie Review, Halifax Chronicle Herald, Saint John Telegraph Journal, Hamilton Spectator*, the *Times Literary Supplement*, the *Vancouver Province*, the *Winnipeg Free Press, Queen's Quarterly, Atlantic Monthly* and *Foreign Affairs*.

It was felt a further increase in meal charges could make cost of a lunch unattractive, particularly if a member partakes of one or two drinks. The cost of a lunch under these circumstances could go as high as $6.50 a person.

Hot free Hors d'oeuvres to be served in the main lounge between 5 and 7 p.m. [Another disappointment, though Pearson added: "Now that Hors d'oeuvres are being passed as opposed to members helping themselves,

attendance might improve, inviting the ladies to partici-
pate." No such luck — Service was discontinued
February 1971].

1971:
The question of an alternative site for the Rideau Club,
in the event of a forced move in the near future, was
discussed. It was suggested the Committee look at a
building in Lower Town now owned by the National
Capital Commission, and discreet inquiries were authorized. [Site was too far from the present flow of our
Patrons.]

The number of resignations causes concern, some
because they were not satisfied with the facilities offered
by the Club. A substantial loss in members is noted over
past few years.

September 23, 1971:
In an effort to improve the quality of food on a daily
basis, the House Committee decided to reduce the
number of choices available on the menu each day, and
the Committee of Management agrees.

After an examination of the functions of the various
bars, it became apparent that one of the delays at the
main bar was a result of specially mixed drinks which
were time consuming to produce. To discourage the
ordering of more exotic drinks their price will be
increased to $1.50 each.

Also on September 23, 1971, a Happy Hour experiment was authorized by President Pearson, but it failed to
boost business at the bar.

On October 19, 1971, Mr Pearson, as President,
agreed to make the Club available to the Soviet Chairman
Alexei Kosygin for a luncheon with 130 guests. All booze
was from Russia, along with four types of smoked fish, and

red and black caviar. Chef Emile Bezen spoke Russian.
Chairman Kosygin arrived at 12.12, Prime Minister and
Mrs Trudeau at 12.25. Shortly after three o'clock it was
all over. Kosygin's speech was translated into French
only, and after leaving the Club, Kosygin was attacked
by a protester on Parliament Hill, but was unharmed,
though ruffled.

January 20, 1972:

The Chairman of the Special Events Committee said he
was unable to obtain a guest speaker for the annual Club
dinner scheduled for next month. President Pearson said
he would approach the Prime Minister to see if he could
attend as the Guest of Honour for this occasion.
(Trudeau said no.) [On April 17, 1975, the question of
membership for Prime Minister Trudeau was raised again
and it was suggested that it be deferred for the new
Membership Committee to look into the possibility of
the Prime Minister and ministers of his cabinet becoming members of the Rideau Club.]

February 24, 1972:

Chairman Pearson pointed out we are losing approxi-
mately $12,000 a year by operating the Ladies' Section.
The bulk of the loss is incurred during the evening, since
we serve on an average of 11 dinners per night and
require a staff of 10 people to operate the Club during
this period. In other words, the Club loses over $2.00 for
every meal served in the Ladies Dining Room during the
evening meal. Serious consideration to be given to
closing the Club at 5 p.m. and operating as a luncheon
club only.

March 30, 1972:

The Secretary was requested to scan the local papers for
new appointments to the capital and report them to the
Membership Committee as possible candidates for
membership.

October 25, 1972:

Charles Lynch agreed to be the guest speaker at the annual Club dinner scheduled for Thursday, December 14, and it was suggested Mr Lester B. Pearson be asked to introduce Mr Lynch.

December 7, 1972:

Mr Pearson is ill; the President had approached Dr C.J. Mackenzie and he had accepted to introduce the guest speaker.

The President said that he felt that since this was a private Club dinner, there should not be any newspaper reporting of Mr Lynch's speech. The President said he had spoken to Mr Lynch who said that because of his connection with the Press, he himself could not restrict any reporting of his speech, but he would not object to the Club making this restriction. It was the opinion of the board that the President should request the Members present at the Dinner to treat Mr Lynch's remarks as being off the record to allow Mr Lynch more freedom of expression.

November 21, 1972:

The Chairman of the Special Events Committee reported that they expect between 155 and 165 people to attend the function tomorrow night and that Mr Charles Lynch had agreed to act as auctioneer for the sale of surplus Club furniture. [The auction of the Club furniture was deemed highly successful since the Club received some $1,381.00.]

Interesting to note that over a century before, under date of July 23, 1869, the records show that proceeds of the sale of Club furniture amounted to $1,341, less $33.52 for the auctioneer and an additional $20 because proceeds of the sale were not what had been anticipated. They must have had a better auctioneer!

December 7, 1972:

The question of increasing the minimum charge for food services in the Dining Room being increased to $1.50 to be considered at a future meeting when more information will be available. Present minimum is $1.00. Agreed it should remain so.

The Club Steward, Mr Ronald M. Small, is retiring at his own request after nine months service. It was agreed that a separation allowance was not necessary, but he would be permitted to retain his uniform since it would not fit the new Steward, G.J. Mignault.

President Pearson's signature bears witness to all of the foregoing, though his own comments are unrecorded.

GG's and PM's

*T*here was a time when the Rideau Club was virtually a branch office of Rideau Hall. But times change.

The last Governor General who used the Club was Michener, following a long line of viceroys who represented the Queen in the original sense of perpetuating the British connection.

In Ottawa, from its beginnings as a capital, the British presence was asserted by the Canadian counterparts of the institutions of the Raj: Parliament, a copy of Westminster in its rituals; a Governor General; the British High Commission; armed forces, modelled on the British pattern; the rituals of the law courts; the street names (Queen, Wellington, Dalhousie, even the latter-day Queensway); and those names taken from the French word for "curtain" — Rideau Hall, the Rideau Canal, and the Rideau Club. All were responses to the call of Empire, echoes of Sir John A.'s cry: "A British subject I was born, a British subject I will die."

The Rideau Club sent its members and their sons off to fight beside the British in two World Wars as readily as they had gone, earlier, to the Boer War and before that to flush out Louis Riel and his rebels in the West.

From August 17, 1885:
The dinner to be given to Major General Frederick Middleton by the President and Members of the Club, on the occasion of his safe return from his command in the North West Territories and victory in the Battle of Batoche, should be held on Tuesday the 18th Instant, at 7.30 o'clock.

Like its fellow clubs across the land, the Rideau Club was a bastion of the "ready, aye, ready" syndrome, but it changed with the times, more rapidly than the rest, after agonies of conscience whose scars were cauterized by the flames that burned the clubhouse down.

Jules Léger, who succeeded Roland Michener as Governor General, and who traced his office back to New France, felt ill at ease in the Rideau Club, as did most French Canadians. Yet, earlier, Governor General Georges Vanier was able to relax in the Club, having spent most of his professional life in the military atmosphere of the Canadian army, so determinedly Anglo. And the first Canadian Governor General, Vincent Massey, was described as more British than the British. "He does make one feel such a peasant," a British lord once said. He might have wished the Rideau Club to be more up to the mark on the patterns set in London.

Edward Schreyer, as Governor General, was little disposed to clubdom, much less towards the Rideau Club which, to most New Democrats, was a symbol of elitism and capitalist exploitation, the refuge of the hated bosses and the denizens of the boardrooms.

And the advent of Jeanne Sauvé as Governor General did little to re-introduce the vice-regal presence into the Club. When she was Speaker of the House of Commons, Madame Sauvé had supported a boycott of the Club because of its discrimination against women.

But the Rideau Club remained on speaking terms with the courtiers of Rideau Hall, no matter what the chill at the top. The same could not be said about relations with latter-day Prime Ministers, starting with John Diefenbaker.

Before the great Prairie populist became Prime Minister, every PM from Sir John A. onwards had been a member of the Rideau Club, along with most members of their cabinets. Some, like Sir Wilfrid Laurier and Louis St Laurent, were not regular patrons, but Sir Robert Borden was President following his term as Prime Minister, a pattern that would be followed by Lester B. Pearson who was Club President in 1971.

All Prime Ministers, as all Governors General back to Confederation, have their photographs lining the walls of the Club's entrance hall whether they might like it or not.

One who would chuckle would be Diefenbaker, having shunned the Rideau Club for its discrimination, just as he would not set foot in other clubs for the same reason.

When Diefenbaker came to power, he ruled the Rideau Club off-limits for government functions and discouraged government-sponsored memberships for ministers and for their deputies, who during the long years of Liberal rule had come to regard the Club as a natural perquisite of power. Diefenbaker once exulted, from his prime ministerial office on the Hill, that "at last, I can look down on the Rideau Club!"

Though some politicians and deputy ministers continued their memberships on their own account, the Diefenbaker boycott cost the Club both in membership fees and in its long-time association with the levers of power.

As Prime Minister, Pearson tried to restore the Rideau Club to government favour, for official functions as well as memberships, but even though he persevered to the extent of eventually becoming Club President, the old political ties were never restored. "No votes there," said one Old Pol.

Pierre Elliott Trudeau regarded the Club not only as an obstacle to his declared objective of bilingualizing the nation's capital, but also as a tangible symbol of English-speaking domination, as obvious as the British Crown itself.

Trudeau had two additional reasons to shun the Rideau Club and to encourage his ministers and their deputies to do the same.

One was the ban on full-time membership for women.

The other was that at the time he was the least club-bable of men, disliking especially, as he would put it, being in the company of Club members who never stop talking or of sombre-faced neanderthals speaking only in grunts and growls. Even in his beloved Montreal he shunned clubs where affluence and clubdom went hand-in-hand.

After women were admitted, Trudeau did attend one office party on the Rideau Club premises, feigning horror and talking in mock whispers "so as not to wake the dead." Within a week of the Trudeau visit, the Club burned down. In recent years, however, Pierre Trudeau has been noticed occasionally in the new Club premises, preferring a small table for two overlooking Parliament Hill.

Joe Clark, who was Prime Minister at the time of the fire, like Diefenbaker never joined the Club, perhaps feeling membership would damage the image he cultivated as "the man from High River".

And when Brian Mulroney became Prime Minister, he seemed to prefer the Press Club to the Rideau Club, sometimes showing up there unannounced to have lunch with his deputy Don Mazankowski, and then working the dining room with handshakes and one-liners, behaviour that draws raised eyebrows even at today's democratized Rideau Club, where table-hopping is almost unknown. One joke at the Press Club is that whenever Mulroney comes in, 200 other diners put "lunch with PM" on their expense accounts. At the Rideau Club expense accounts are much used, but never talked about.

Mostly, Mulroney and his ministers lunch and dine elsewhere, as was the case with the Trudeau team. The many dining rooms on the Parliamentary premises, plus the opulent official dining room at External Affairs headquarters in the Lester B. Pearson building, give politicians a wide choice. Even the Supreme Court Justices, who long had their own exclusive table at the Rideau Club, now have their own courthouse dining room. And in addition to all the embassies that offer hospitality to the powerful, Ottawa has an impressive and growing list of good restaurants, whose prices are quite similar to those of the Rideau Club.

In its glory days as a seat of political power in Ottawa, the Rideau Club offered some of the worst food in the town, if not in the country — the only saving graces being the wheel of Stilton laced with port and the marvellous meat pies. In its new incarnation, the Club offers some of the finest fare anywhere — inspired, it is said, because following the fire, Club members were given privileges in the *Cercle Universitaire*, an offshoot of the University of Ottawa and the first club in the country to offer French cuisine in all its glory. After tasting such Gallic delights, Rideau Club members could never go back to the dreary nosh of old — and a revolution of rising expectations transformed not only the food but every aspect of the

Rideau Club reborn, in which even Francophones could feel *chez nous*, gastronomically and bilingually speaking.

Whether more was gained than lost in the transformation is a moot point still discussed in whispers in the more remote corners of the new Club premises.

"I see you're letting in the riffraff," said one elder of the Rideau Club, himself the third-generation beneficiary of a timber fortune, upon reading the notice that a prominent Ottawa tradesman had been admitted to membership.

Who Needs a Club, Anyway?

*T*hat old protester was a voice from the past, a defender of a lost cause in a club increasingly given over to gatherings of captains of business and industry, to power lunches and power dinners, a hotbed of lobbying, of deals and rumours of deals, a club whose out-of-town members list includes a horde of corporate chairmen and presidents, obliged to take out membership because the Rideau Club does not exchange reciprocal privileges with their home-town affiliations, however grand.

At noon, the Club foyer looks more like the site of a yuppy convention than the old, crusty venue of clubland; and the once-sacrosanct Reading Room, where hardly anyone glances now at the ironed copies of the born-again *Times* of London, echoes with the gossip not of politics but of the marketplace. The once-famous Rideau Club dry martinis, served by the pitcherful to members who sometimes had to drink them through straws to bypass the trembles, have given way to mineral water or that non-alcoholic variant of the Bloody Mary, the Bloody Shame, or Bloody Shame's lighter cousin, the Virgin Caesar.

And cigar smoke curls no more into the woodwork, nor into the drapes and upholstery, dramatic in colours that would have struck the founding fathers blind.

But, before saying goodbye to clubdom in its old form, let's dwell a little longer on what it was and continued to be in the Rideau Club well into the sixties, and still can be found in some surviving clubs across the land where the slap of progress is felt less sharply than in poll-crazed, protest-ridden and lobby-happy Ottawa.

One English clubman said happiness was Pears soap and proper hand towels.

Club President Guy Roberge, in a toast to British High Commissioner Sir John Ford and Lady Ford in 1981, put it this way:

> Naturally, we would have preferred to be your hosts at our ancient Club which had much in common with the Clubs on Pall Mall, their common rooms, lunch tables and, more important, their silence rooms. . . .
>
> Anthony Sampson, in his book *Anatomy of Britain Today*, said: "Clubs are an unchallenged English invention, and they remain one of our most successful exports."
>
> We intend to continue that English invention in our new home, where we hope to have the pleasure of welcoming you. . . . That English invention has been a source of pleasure for which the Members of the Rideau are thankful, and of which they are proud.
>
> One of the greatest among your Secretaries of State for Foreign Affairs, Lord Palmerston, is supposed to have said:
>
> "Dining is the soul of diplomacy.". . .

"Dining — to a Club Member — is the soul of friendship."

Generations of nobby Brits have had clubdom instilled into their minds and bones, synonymous with privilege, nobility, place. Hence the decline of the clubs has been an almost essential element in the weakening of the British class system, that stratification of society that never did quite implant itself in Canada where status has had more to do with money than with lineage. All fortunes may be assumed to have had something to do with pillage, but the old ones have tended to look down on the new, forgetting their own origins under the cloak of a pseudo-aristocracy.

Like the Established Church and the private schools, the English-style clubs, or at least the patterns they set, spread their influence with the Empire, except that in the colonies they were more a veneer than an essential ingredient of society.

There are 218 urban and country clubs in Canada, and that is just the official total according to the membership list of the Canadian Society of Club Managers, where professional club management is understood to be Big Business.

Ontario leads the list with 84, followed by Alberta with 46, Quebec with 28, Manitoba and Saskatchewan with 20, the national capital with 18, British Columbia with 15 and Nova Scotia with seven.

There are some — the Garrison Club in Quebec, the Union Club in Saint John, and others, in Victoria, St. John's, Medicine Hat — whose origins reach back into the nineteenth century.

In Canada the kind of clubdom involved in our story includes chiefly the Rideau Club in Ottawa, the Albany, National, Toronto, Ontario and York in Toronto, the Hamilton Club, the London Club, the Manitoba in Winnipeg, the Ranchmen's and Petroleum clubs in Calgary, the Edmonton Club, the Vancouver and Terminal City clubs in Vancouver, and the Halifax Club in Halifax.

Unlike the country clubs, the golf clubs, the curling clubs, the Legion halls and the other single- or multi-purpose watering holes, these were the clubs established and operated on the British pattern, with no declared purpose other than conviviality and accepted qualifications for membership, with privacy and discretion as watch-words. If there was a common thread of roguishness, it was gambling: playing cards for stakes that often ran high.

"Clubbable" is a word from Edwardian times, though the Rideau goes back to the middle of Victoria's reign. It is a word that had a favourable ring in upper-class ears, but was pejorative to the rest, except for those whom we would now describe as upwardly mobile, who aspired to club membership as a mark of success.

For clubbable men in the old sense, no aspirations were necessary. The club came by right, as naturally as the

94

houses, the country places, the coaches or automobiles, even the private railway cars. The club was a place of immunity from what now is known as the rat race.

For the powerful, the club was both a refuge from business, when it suited them, and a place to do deals on the side — to plan a fishing trip, or a takeover, or the building of a mansion grander than one's neighbour's.

And above all, the club was where men congregated without women — an extension of that musty old practice, still observed in some of the grander Ottawa embassies (housed in those same big mansions of old), where the ladies move to the "withdrawing room", leaving men to their cigars, their port, their gossip and their jokes, usually as stale as the air they breathe. Club jokes tend not to be thigh-slappers. The Ottawa outpost on the international joke network in Ottawa is the Press Club, not the Rideau Club.

The clubman has been lampooned, from Shakespeare through Gilbert and Sullivan, Shaw, Coward, Wodehouse and a host of cartoonists, some of the most brilliant of them Canadian. The precursors of the clubman species could be found in ancient Greece and Rome, and doubtless in the Egypt of the Pharaohs, and their gradual extinction seems worth at least a footnote in history, and a word in their defence.

In a wobbly world, they stood for something as a few of them are standing yet, pretending the institutions have stood the test of time, which most of them have not.

Some are venerated, none more than Roly Michener, his polish acquired in his years in Britain after his Alberta upbringing. Yet Michener emerged not unduly "Limeytized" — the British influence was tempered by his broad family connections in the United States and the roots he put down in Toronto, building that breadth in him that led to his political success and his ease with High Places.

On his way out on that fateful last day, Mr Michener passed the little side chamber, known as "the Strangers' Room", dedicated to the confinement of visitors awaiting hosts. Most English and Canadian clubs had such places of incarceration for outsiders, just as most clubs refused to divulge to telephone callers whether or not a member was in attendance. Sometimes it was not so much attendance as sanctuary, especially if a club had bedrooms, as the Rideau Club did before they became so scruffy they had to be walled off.

The rooms were home to bachelor members, some of whom were said, as the *Globe and Mail* reported, to have smuggled women into their top-floor chambers, though the Club records avoid any incriminating references in conformity with the custom of regarding women as unmentionable. More often, the rooms, with their commanding view of Parliament Hill, provided a resting place for Club members who had been thrown out of their homes, or had fled. But the rental of these rooms could be revoked for transgression of Club rules, as the following excerpts from the minutes show:

October 12, 1954:

Brigadier Mortimore reported that he had received a complaint that unbecoming language had been used by a tenant member to certain members of the staff while on duty. Moved by Mr O'Brien and seconded by Mr Elderkin that he be advised that he was suspended from membership of the Club as from present date, that he must vacate his room by October 15 and that should he fail to give a satisfactory account of his conduct to the Committee by Oct. 22 he would be expelled from the Club.

Myrna Kean, bell girl, confirmed a remark made to her by the member in the reading room.

And this, from April 23, 1956:

John W. Hughson complained of embarrassment caused to his wife while a guest at the Club by the impolite conduct of that same tenant member. He is to be advised to vacate the bedroom at present occupied by him at end of the three-month period. His plea to remain is granted, at $75.00 a month.

Rental of rooms ended in 1967, because of dilapidation and lack of patronage.

That Old Diehard: Anti-Semitism

*R*equirements for Club
memberships vary, and money is sometimes the least
important consideration.

At Rome's aristocratic club, La Caccia, it is a matter
of pride that the club blackballed J. Paul Getty when the
American was the world's richest man. Canadian men's
clubs used the blackball without restriction well into this
century, the Rideau Club among them, as we shall see. It
was a simpler matter in the days when everybody who was
anybody knew everybody else who was, and had strong
views about who wasn't — not to mention what was, and
what wasn't, done, at least in public.

At the Rideau Club, Jews and women knew they need
not apply.

"It is seriously damaging to my reputation to suggest
that I would so demean myself as to seek admission to a
club which it was well known did not then welcome Jewish
members. In fact, I had no desire to become a member of
the Rideau Club."

The Governor of the Bank of Canada, Louis
Rasminsky, was incensed when he wrote those words in

1975, 11 years after he had been a central figure in the Club's effort to rid itself of anti-Semitism.

Today, the redoubtable Rasminsky still recalls the events with emotion, and still insists that there should be no mincing of words — to him, "racism" is too vague a word for what it was then, and remains, in spots, today. "Call it anti-Semitism," he says, with the vigour of a man who has fought against it all his business, social and leisure life. He knows how.

He was the nation's top banker, directing the course of the economy, his signature on the currency, his policies influencing its value, often amid raging political controversy.

But he could not join the Rideau Club, the chief centre of power off Parliament Hill. And it was his impression that no Jew could, though one Jewish Member of Parliament was said to have been accepted because nobody knew he was a Jew, and author Peter C. Newman achieved membership on the same misapprehension — the wielders of the blackball ballots didn't notice.

Within the Club, the winning battle against the blackball was fought in 1964, amid salvos of publicity that very nearly put the kibosh on the whole thing.

What caused Louis Rasminsky's 1975 flare-up was this reference in Peter Newman's book *The Canadian Establishment*: "One successful assault on club anti-Semitism took place at the Rideau Club in the summer of

1964. Louis Rasminsky, then Governor of the Bank of Canada, had already been denied entry."

In a letter to publisher Jack McClelland, Rasminsky said: "The inescapable implication of the statement that I was 'denied' entry before 1964 is that I sought entry. This is untrue."

The Governor of the Bank of Canada, having said he would not so demean himself, and that he had no desire to become a member of a Club that discriminated against Jews, went on to explain what really happened:

> It was only when a group of enlightened members, Arnold Heeney, Blair Fraser, Nik Monserrat and Davey Dunton, approached me in 1964 and solicited my help in changing what they regarded as an intolerable position, that I gave consideration to allowing my name to stand.
>
> Even then, I was worried about the possibility that the four people they approached would become "token Jews", but after further discussions and the change in the rules governing the admission of members I agreed to have my name go forward.
>
> I have no doubt that with this knowledge of the facts you will regret that your firm has published the false and damaging statement of which I complain, and will wish to minimize the damage that has been done to me by taking appropriate steps to that end.

In fact, Rasminsky received an apology from both McClelland and Newman, and the offending passage was removed from subsequent editions of *The Canadian Establishment*.

Rasminsky recalls that he turned down the initial 1964 entreaties that he permit his name to stand, fearing that the Rideau Club would bypass the blackball to let four Jews in, and then quietly restore the barrier, while pointing to its token Jewish members to deny that there was prejudice.

Top Mandarin Heeney, Top Journalist Fraser, Top Novelist Monserrat and Top Educator Dunton went back to seek a way that would satisfy the Bank of Canada Governor and his fellow Jews. They realized they would have to eliminate the blackball, the ancient system of membership application processing that encouraged bigotry to flourish in secrecy. The system had been invented to control obstreperous politicians in the Athenian democracy. In clubland (and elsewhere) it was used to reject "undesirable" membership candidates. In the old Rideau Club, members voted secretly on each new applicant. One negative vote would cancel ten affirmative ones, and 15 negative votes would exclude a candidate, regardless of how many affirmative votes were cast.

One member who helped the Heeney group find a solution was Denis Coolican, now a past president of the Club, who says he was drawn into the fray by the sudden realization that his friend and contemporary, David Golden, was a Jew.

Coolican had been vaguely aware that there were no Jewish Club members, without worrying why. "I always thought," he recalls, "the criterion for approving membership in the Rideau Club was whether or not you would have the fellow in your own home." To Coolican, Dave Golden passed that test.

Agitation brought to light that many Rideau Club members were troubled by the ancient prejudice, but knew it applied in clubs across the land, and at many of the best resorts, though seldom on a formal basis. Some places posted "Restricted" signs, and everybody knew what they meant. But city clubs didn't do that. They didn't have to.

Coolican and his fellows set out to put things right, and before the job was finished the Rideau Club, and along with it the leading members of Ottawa's vigorous Jewish community, would be put through the publicity wringer, and the emotional wringer as well.

The year 1964 was the eve of the Club's 100th birthday, a time to celebrate a century of quiet fellowship and high old times, in the best of company, when words like WASP and Yuppie were unknown, and words like Jew were rarely spoken in polite society other than in lamenting Nazi bestiality, now 20 years past and just beginning to be labelled "Holocaust".

The membership blackball was taken for granted, dating back as it did to Sir John A. and the founders. Its original purpose was to provide a general form of exclusivity, but its effect was to institutionalize anti-Semitism (and anti-feminism).

The origins of anti-Semitism are clouded by time, but its effects were everywhere, in the new world as in the old. In Canada, they were present in all levels of everyday life. And in the city clubs, where high society and big business met, the rules were understood, and even codified. In Moncton, N.B., my own father, enlightened in other matters, told me off for buying underwear in "a Jew store". That was in 1960, and he was not mollified by the fact that the label was Stanfield's.

In 1964, the Rideau Club rules did not specify, in so many words, that women and Jews need not apply.

What the rules of that year said was that the membership committee could permit members to entertain ladies in the Club after 7 o'clock in the evening, and could at any time withdraw or suspend such permission, either in whole or in part, without assigning any cause or reason.

The other control was a requirement that each candidate for membership needed 21 votes in his favour to be elected, and could be excluded by one negative in every ten votes of the total, and that, in any case, a total of 15 negative votes meant exclusion.

If the candidate's proposer and seconder desired, a second ballot could be taken in the same manner on another of the regular ballot days, when the full membership put their voting slips in the box.

Any candidate blackballed on the second ballot under the one-to-ten formula would be ineligible for proposal again for a period of one year.

And any candidate twice proposed and twice negatived was ineligible for life.

The first major move to end the blackball had been made in 1957, when it was proposed to eliminate the ballot by members, replacing it by forming a membership committee whose responsibility it would be to elect candidates for ordinary membership.

The committee would be composed of past presidents and past management committee members, as well as active members of the management committee.

Notices of nomination would be posted on the Club bulletin board, and any member could offer written comments. The management committee would "consider each candidate and take such action as they deem fit to see that an adequate number of members know the candidate and that he is otherwise suitable, after which the nomination would go to a membership committee which would vote by a show of hands, for or against, admission requiring a four-fifths vote of members present."

"After considerable discussion," say the minutes briskly, "the amendments were put to a vote of the Members present at the special general meeting, and on a count of hands were declared rejected. The meeting then adjourned."

The leaders of the 1964 uprising knew all that, and so did every member of the Rideau Club, though nobody talked about it.

Only a few knew that Lawrence Freiman, Ottawa's merchant prince, philanthropist and patron of the arts, a leading member of the international Jewish community, had unknowingly been scorched by the Rideau Club blackball when Duncan McTavish proposed putting him up for membership without his knowledge.

McTavish, national President of the Liberal Party and prominent Ottawa lawyer, sounded out the proposal and was advised: "That's fine, but he won't make it. . . ." Mr Freiman had a host of friends and admirers in the Club, but not enough to counter the weighted prejudice against Jews.

Coolican recalls telling Arnold Heeney: "Hell, this is no good. I am appalled about this."

He offered to organize the Club, which meant polling the full membership one by one, to see where the blackball votes were, and then ensuring that enough positive votes were cast to overcome the opposition.

"I will second it," was Heeney's reply. "Not only will I support it, but if Dave Golden and the others don't make it, I will resign from the Club."

Coolican said he didn't propose to go to such lengths, and Heeney replied, "Well, I do. If we don't rebel against this kind of thing the first thing you will know they'll be blackballing Irish Catholics."

"I got the message," says Irish Catholic Coolican, "and we set to work immediately." Heeney and fellow mandarin Norman Robertson took the lead.

There were consultations with several past presidents of the Club, including Mr Justice Douglas Abbott of the Supreme Court. Mr Justice Abbott recommended against trying to "organize" a positive vote of the membership, even though Mr Coolican had a feeling he knew where every blackball vote was; as he puts it today, "some of them were and are my friends."

Instead, Mr Justice Abbott proposed to deal with the problem the way it had been handled in the University Club in Montreal: change the voting procedure, and quietly abolish the blackball in the process. That could be done by a majority vote of a full meeting of the membership called for the purpose, with no weighted voting.

But both Mr Justice Abbott and Dr Norman McKenzie agreed it would be unfair to ask one Jew to stand without some other candidates beside him. So four prominent members of the Jewish community were approached, told what was afoot, and invited to let their names stand in nomination. They were Lawrence Freiman, his brother-in-law lawyer Bernard Alexandor, Bank of Canada Governor Louis Rasminsky, and David Golden.

They agreed, and a special general meeting was called by written notice from the president, which included this explanation:

> The ballot system which has been in use since the founding of the Club has some disadvantages, one of which is that it does enable any small organized group to decide who shall not be elected and this is achieved under a cloak of secrecy.
>
> Furthermore it is open to doubt whether the majority of members give much serious thought to the election of new members. Somewhere between 50 and 90 members usually vote but it is not thought that the gentlemen being voted on are known to the majority of the voters — they accept the judgment of the Committee or that of the proposer and seconder.
>
> Thus while balloting does not necessarily result in careful selection by the majority it can lead to a type of exclusiveness which is inimical to the Club's best interests and desired only by a few.
>
> It becomes increasingly important that careful consideration be given to the selection of each new member and it has been suggested that this might be achieved by changing from the ballot system to a system embracing a selection committee, which has proved both popular and successful in certain other clubs comparable to ours.

The moment the notice was circulated it was in the Ottawa newspapers, with headlines blaring the names of the four Jewish nominees who were challenging the blackball.

An emergency meeting of the Committee of Management was called under the chairmanship of Norman

Robertson. The minutes tell the story, under the date of
July 29, 1964:

> A special meeting of the Committee of Management
> was held this date at the Rideau Club at 12.30 p.m.
> There were present Mr Heeney, Mr O'Brien, Mr
> Perley-Robertson, Dr Trueman and Mr White with
> Mr Norman A. Robertson in the Chair.
>
> This special meeting was called to discuss the recent
> articles appearing in local and out of town newspapers
> concerning the nominations for membership of Messrs
> Alexandor, Golden, Freiman and Rasminsky.
>
> Messrs Heeney and Robertson informed the Com-
> mittee that these misleading and grossly inaccurate
> articles had caused considerable embarrassment to the
> gentlemen in question and that both Mr Freiman and
> Mr Rasminsky were in the process of requesting that
> their names be withdrawn from the list of nominations.
> In fact, the Secretary had just received a letter from
> Mr Freiman requesting that his name be withdrawn.
>
> Mr Heeney was of the opinion that the Committee
> should write to each of the gentlemen in question and
> presented a draft letter for the Committee's consider-
> ation. After a lengthy discussion it was agreed that the
> Secretary should write a letter to the four gentlemen
> expressing the Committee's feelings regarding the recent
> articles.
>
> The Committee also expressed their concern over the
> fact that privileged information concerning Club busi-
> ness was being communicated to the press and were of
> the opinion that members of the press who are members
> of the Club should be requested to appear before the
> Committee to be censured for their actions and explain
> the circumstances.

And two days later, the Committee met again:

> A special meeting of the Committee of Management was held this date at the Rideau Club at 12.30 p.m. There were present Mr Heeney, Mr O'Brien, Mr Perley-Robertson, Mr Robertson, Dr Trueman and Mr White with Mr Denis A. Ross in the Chair.
>
> The meeting was called to discuss what further action should be taken regarding the Club's position in respect to the unfavourable publicity received as a result of the recent newspaper articles.
>
> It was decided that the Secretary should write a letter to the editors of the *Citizen* and *Journal* requesting that the contents of the letter sent to Messrs Alexandor, Golden, Freiman and Rasminsky be made public and that a copy of the letters to the editors be sent with a covering letter to the publishers of each newspaper for their personal attention. The question of a meeting with the members of the press should be the subject of a further meeting.

The story had been published first in the *Citizen*, and picked up by papers across the country. It included a paragraph that stated: "It is understood that Mr Freiman, whose family have long been leading citizens of Ottawa, has been nominated for Rideau Club membership twice before. Both times he was 'blackballed,' apparently because he is Jewish."

This reference so outraged Mr Freiman that he ceased to speak to the then-newly-appointed editor of the *Citizen*, Christopher Young, whose position was made even more uncomfortable by the fact that the Freiman store was the paper's biggest local advertiser.

The *Citizen* subsequently published this apology:

The *Citizen* erroneously reported that Lawrence Freiman, head of the A.J. Freiman department stores, had twice been nominated and rejected for membership in the Rideau Club.

This is not the case. Mr Freiman had previously been asked to allow his name to stand for membership in the Rideau Club but had refused. His current nomination is the first time that he has agreed to let his name stand.

The *Citizen* regrets any embarrassment that this report may have caused.

And the paper published the letter written by Club Secretary W.E. Milner to Messrs Alexandor, Golden, Freiman and Rasminsky:

I have been instructed by the committee of the Rideau Club to express to you their deep regret at the misleading and grossly inaccurate reports which have appeared recently in certain newspapers concerning your nomination for membership.

It is, of course, quite untrue that any initiative was taken on your part to seek membership; the proposal was put forward and supported by members as required by the Club's constitution. It is entirely false that Mr Freiman had been nominated previously.

It is the sincere hope of all members of the committee that you will not permit this unhappy incident to interfere with your name coming forward for consideration in the usual course. The Club will be closed for the normal summer vacation over the next three weeks, but very soon after it is reopened, the membership committee will be reporting on current nominations. At least until that time, the committee urges you to allow matters to stand as they are.

Club members were as good as their word.

The August break had hardly ended when the issue was addressed, on September 1:

A meeting of the Committee of Management at 12.45 p.m. Present, Mr Coolican, Mr Gill, Vice Ad. Grant, Mr Heeney, Mr Maclaren, Mr Perley-Robertson, Mr Robertson, Mr Ross and Mr White with the president, Rear Ad. W.B. Creery, in the Chair. The minutes of the meetings of July 21, 29 and 31 were read and adopted subject to the deletion of the word "censure" in reference to members of the press and substitute the words "explain the circumstances". . . .

The names and particulars of candidates being proposed for ordinary membership were circulated to all ordinary members of the Club. Several members exercised their option and wrote or telephoned the Committee expressing their views. Of the more than 20 letters and phone calls received, eight members wished to go on record objecting either to the system of selection or to certain candidates proposed.

These gentlemen were advised that their objections would be discussed at this meeting. The remaining letters were unanimous in their support of all candidates proposed and in particular those of the Jewish faith.

The letters of objection were read and discussed and the President was of the opinion that there was no valid reason given in any of these letters that would constitute bona fide objections to the candidates proposed.

However, if some of the members object to the new system of selection of members, they are within their rights under the constitution to request a special general meeting of the Club on a requisition signed by ten or more ordinary members.

The chairman of the Membership Committee made his report to the Committee. The President then called for a vote by open ballot and the following gentlemen

Scarred reminder of the old Club
(*Media Production Services, University of Ottawa*)

After the fire — the image remains
(*Photograph by Nickolas Haramis*)

The new entrance hall, under the eyes of Governors General and Prime Ministers

(Photograph by Rupert Westmaas)

An impressive entrance — the front lobby
(John Evans Photography Ltd., Ottawa)

The old Club was
reduced to rubble, but
the crest survived intact
(*Media Production Services,
University of Ottawa*)

The Presidents Board —
history at a glance
(*Media Production Services,
University of Ottawa*)

PRESIDENTS OF THE RIDEAU CLUB

The Loggia — the best verandah in town
(*John Evans Photography Ltd., Ottawa*)

A sense of quiet — the Reading Room
(John Evans Photography Ltd., Ottawa)

The new Board Room — masterpieces by Karsh (east wall)

(Photograph by Malak, Ottawa)

The new Board Room — masterpieces by Karsh (west wall)

(*Photograph by Malak, Ottawa*)

A new elegance and a new Dining Room
(*Photograph by Rupert Westmaas*)

The Bar — a popular meeting place

(John Evans Photography Ltd., Ottawa)

A welcoming fire in the main lounge, fifteen floors up
(*Media Production Services, University of Ottawa*)

Tapestry, sculpture, jellybeans — familiar sights at the new Club
(*Media Production Services, University of Ottawa*)

The final result — three glorious tables
(Photograph by Rupert Westmaas)

A privileged view from the main lounge
(*Media Production Services, University of Ottawa*)

A different perspective on the Peace Tower
(John Evans Photography Ltd., Ottawa)

Charles Lynch with a stone carving — the Billiards Trophy donated by Judge J.D. Hyndman — which was salvaged from the fire

(Ottawa Citizen photograph by Ron Poling)

were unanimously approved for ordinary membership: Bernard Alexandor, Q.C., lawyer: Proposer, C.J. Mackenzie, seconder Hon. Mr Justice D.C. Abbott. Lawrence Freiman, Executive: Proposer, Comm. F.J.D. Pemberton, seconder J. Ross Tolmie, Q.C. David A. Golden, Air Industries Assoc. of Canada: Proposer, A. Davidson Dunton, seconder, Dr O.M. Solandt. Louis Rasminsky, Governor, Bank of Canada: Proposer, Blair Fraser, seconder, A. Davidson Dunton.

The question of how to deal with the members of the press who are members of the Club was again discussed, and it was agreed that, rather than bring members of the press before the Committee, the President should personally speak to the publishers of the *Journal* and the *Citizen* expressing the concern of the Committee that private business of the Club is being made public causing considerable embarrassment to the individuals reported upon and also to the Club.

It is hoped that by this personal liaison the President will be able to get the assurance of the publishers that further publicity of private business will be avoided. It was further agreed that the names of the candidates approved for membership would not be posted on the notice board until after the President had spoken to the publishers. The letter to each candidate advising him of his election would however be sent out in the usual manner.

The House Committee was then requested to look into the possibility of a new source of supply for oysters....

Coolican recalls today that the diehards told him they were against abolishing the blackball, no matter what happened. "They didn't explain, and I didn't. We didn't have to. We knew where we stood, and we stayed friends."

Nobody expected, much less wanted, an opening of the floodgates of membership with the lifting of the racial barrier. Here are two subsequent excerpts from the minutes, to show how nominations were dealt with in the wake of the 1964 breakthrough.

December 1, 1966:

The President reported to the Committee that the interpretation of membership by-law by the immediate past president, who introduced it, was that the membership subcommittee shall consider all nominations for membership in the Club and shall report to the Committee of Management as to the eligibility and desirability of the persons as nominated. The Committee as a whole was without question to have discretion in the matter of the suitability of the nominations before their names are posted on the notice board and sent forward to the members for any comment they may wish to make. It was noted that three negative votes within the Committee as a whole exclude a candidate at the time of an election by the Committee.

And in 1967:

In order that more members of the Club and particularly Members of the Committee could meet prospective candidates for membership, it was suggested that the proposer be requested to introduce his candidate to as many members as possible.

The chairman of the Membership Committee said that his Committee had reviewed three applications for ordinary membership that had been deferred from last year and said that his Committee were unanimous in the opinion that approval of these candidates was not in the best interest of the Club. The Committee therefore recommends that the sponsors be requested to withdraw their candidates' names from membership in the Rideau Club. After further discussion, it was agreed that the

Secretary be authorized to approach the sponsors and verbally request them to withdraw their candidates' names. . . .

Since another three gentlemen proposed were not too well known, it was suggested that their names be deferred until their sponsors were able to introduce their candidates to members of the Committee.

Jews, at least, knew they could be put up for membership if they wanted to. The Club had dealt with that matter on its own, and in the process met the objections of John Diefenbaker, though he never bothered to comment, much less patronize the place, and carried to his grave his impression that the Club was a nest of Grits.

Women would have to wait another dozen years for fair and equal treatment, and the Club would feel the wrath of the federal government before the all-male membership caved in, kicking and screaming, while the publicity mills were once again grinding away.

Dressing Up, and Down

*T*he renaissance of Ottawa and of the Rideau Club have gone hand in hand, often involving Club members in great projects, just as in earlier days discussions at the Club had led to the creation of the National Art Gallery, the National Film Board, the Dominion Drama Festival, the Canadian Broadcasting Corporation, the National Archives, the National Capital Commission and the National Arts Centre.

The mix of cultural and social elites was not always an easy one and there were some noisy clashes, the most memorable one involving G. Hamilton Southam, both a patron and participant in the arts.

Mr Southam, a professional diplomat, encouraged the government of Lester B. Pearson to build the National Arts Centre as a centennial project and then became its first Director General. No single project ever did more to improve the ambience of the one-time lumber town and political beehive, putting Ottawa into the mainstream of the lively arts, nationally and worldwide.

The Southam family had made a deeper imprint on Ottawa than on any of the other cities where its newspapers appeared, and G. Hamilton Southam was introduced to the Rideau Club by his publisher father. Hamilton Southam viewed the Rideau Club as a pleasant place to be, until he collided with one of its most rigid rules involving the dress code.

The year was 1969 and the Arts Centre was still in its shakedown phase. A guest artist with the National Ballet had been refused entry into the Centre's restaurant because he was not wearing a cravat, leading Mr Southam to storm at the maitre d': "I now lay down that this is a house for artists and they can come to its restaurants dressed as they please!"

The Rideau Club would prove a tougher nut to crack, as Mr Southam quickly discovered when he tried to introduce his artistic dress standards to the hallowed clubhouse halls.

The Club had had a momentary tolerance for Ascot ties back in the thirties, but the dress code settled back into a pattern that endures to this day, the latest version being:

> For male members, jacket and tie must be worn at all times; turtlenecks, ascots, casual and recreational dress are not acceptable. For lady members, skirts, blouses, jackets, pantsuits and afternoon dress are required. Casual and recreational dress is not acceptable nor, of course, are jeans.

Into the Club strode the Director General of the National Arts Centre with a young guest who had long hair and wore no necktie. This brought a sharp rebuke from the House Committee, informing Mr Southam that he was not to repeat the offence.

The result was this letter of resignation from the offending host:

> My guest, on the occasion in question, had been Mr Stewart Smith, the son of my old friend the Secretary General of the Commonwealth [Mr Arnold Smith]. His dress, in my view, had been neat, orderly and eminently suitable for one of his years and social inclinations. No matter. The Club in its collective wisdom appears to desire a certain conformity in matters of dress — the tie emerges as an essential element of its sumptuary doctrine — and I do not question the Club's right to rule on such matters.
>
> Forgive me if I sound pompous in saying so, but I happen to believe strongly that people shall be judged rather by the views they hold than by the dress they wear. My friend Mr Smith had preferred to wear a loosely-knotted scarf rather than a tie on the occasion in question but our talk over lunch was about goodness, and about what young people would do to make the world better rather than worse.
>
> At the National Arts Centre I have insisted that people should be encouraged to dress as they please, provided they behave with the respect due to the performing arts.... It would be inconsistent, it seems to me, for me to accept at the Club a rule other than the one I have laid down at the Centre.
>
> For the sake of consistency, therefore, and for the sake of a certain decent attitude towards people of talent and rectitude whose views on dress may differ from those of the comfortable majority of my former fellow-members, I am ceasing to regard myself, as of today, as a member of the Rideau Club.

A postscript was added: "[I]t was just when I came home at the end of the war I think that my father put me up [for membership]. Yet I think he would approve of my present gesture."

The response of a member of the House Committee was a brusque "If you want to cut your throat, go ahead."

This was followed by a two-line letter from the Secretary Treasurer of the Club: "As requested in your letter your resignation as an Ordinary Member is accepted with regret."

And that, for ten years, was that, until the rebirth of the Club after the fire, when Hamilton Southam re-joined, bringing with him an associate in the form of designer Giovanni Mowinkel, whose major commission to that date had been Mr Southam's own house at what was arguably the most prestigious private address in Ottawa, 9 Rideau Gate.

Mowinkel won the job of decorating the new Rideau Club, producing another and more public masterpiece. This led to such a flow of commissions that he could not keep pace and wound up in a sordid money squabble with the tenants at 24 Sussex Drive.

Mowinkel returned precipitously to his native Italy where he now has a flourishing practice. He remains in touch with his Canadian admirers, including Hamilton Southam, who recalls fondly a day in London with Mowinkel, purchasing paintings for the new Rideau Club

with insurance money from the lost paintings in the
old clubhouse.

Mr Southam had wanted a female nude to enliven
the new Club bar, but he was overruled by the Arts
Committee, which settled for a stuffed fish caught and
donated by Normandy war hero Col. Charles Petch. But
one London afternoon, Southam and Mowinkel purchased
the entire set of prints that now enliven the panelled walls
of the Club bar, regarded by many as the finest room in
the place.

Other wonders of the Club walls are the huge Karsh
portraits in the Board Room, a breathtaking collection of
the works of the famous photographer and Club member
Yousuf Karsh, selected, mounted and arranged by Karsh
himself. He also presented the Club with portraits of Her
Majesty the Queen and the Duke of Edinburgh, which
Karsh decreed must hang in a certain prominent niche.
There they are, above the fanciest piece of furniture in the
Club, an inlaid table purchased by Mowinkel.

On another wall hang two antique engravings, repre-
senting a re-match of the Plains of Abraham, with French
and English roles reversed by the donors. Club President
Guy Roberge had donated the engraving of the death of
Wolfe, whereupon Hamilton Southam scoured around
until he found a matching one of the death of Montcalm;
so the two heroes of Quebec are shown in their death
throes, side by side, just outside the Sir John A. Macdonald

Room with the Southam plaque on Montcalm and the Roberge plaque on Wolfe.

Arguments about proper attire continue and the porter's desk retains a supply of neckties for potential offenders, while the men's vestibule contains a garment bag, inside which are various-size jackets for those who show up in shirtsleeves. There was a minor crisis in 1975 when the newly unified armed forces introduced a Summer Rig that included neither jackets nor ties. The Club concluded that members of Her Majesty's Forces could enter the premises unimpeded, provided they bore evidence of rank somewhere on their person, preferably on the epaulets.

Also in 1975, in the minutes for January 16:

The President said he had been approached by one of the members complaining that a guest of a member was improperly dressed in that he was wearing an ascot in lieu of a tie. The President asked members of the Board for their opinion, since House Rules say merely that members and guests must be appropriately and properly attired at all times in the Club. It was the opinion of the Board that an ascot should be considered appropriate dress.

In 1989, it was not.

Upstairs, Downstairs

*M*ost of the Club records were destroyed in the fire, but those that survived are truly archival material, the early ones wonderful handwritten accounts of everyday minutiae giving a flavour of the times. From these remnants, here are some nuggets.

1867:

The Committee recommend that a wine bin, capable of holding two bottles in width, and reaching from the floor to the ceiling, be built in the middle of the cellar from east to west, and that all the wine and spirits now in the cellar, except one hogshead of claret and the remainder of the quarter cask of brandy (which is ordered to be returned and exchanged for a cask of better quality) be bottled at once.

Resolved that the bottled sherry is not satisfactory in quality and that the remainder of the same be returned.

Resolved that the use of the Club be allowed for the annual mess dinner of the Civil Service Rifle Regiment, and that the officers of the Privy Council Office Rifle Brigade be requested to renew their subscriptions to the Club.

A member had lately been annoyed at the Club while at dinner by the Steward who persisted in talking on political and other subjects until the member was obliged to request him to retire.

1868:

A barman, waiter and assistant cook will be required during the remainder of the present session of Parliament. The Secretary was therefore instructed to inform the Steward that he must satisfy himself that Beeson and Baker, the applicants, were competent to fill the situations they applied for and, finding them so, that he might employ them for the rest of the session, the barman to be paid $12.00 and the waiter $14.00 per month. The Steward was also authorized to employ the boy Nolan, formerly Billiard marker, as extra waiter, when necessary, at 30 cents per night. . . .

Mr Kennedy, the late Steward, having offered $100 of his son's salary as part payment of his indebtedness to the Club, it was resolved that the offer be accepted and Mr Kennedy called upon to furnish the order necessary to procure the amount from the Accountant of the House of Commons.

October 21, 1869:

The circumstances and condition of the Club do not permit or require the retention of a Secretary, and we are therefore obliged to notify Mr Robert Sinclair that his services cannot be continued.

December 21, 1869:

Mr Sinclair having expressed his wish to be allowed to continue to perform the duty of Secretary without remuneration, it was resolved to accept Mr Sinclair's offer. [Whereafter the handwritten minutes become legible again. Author's note.]

From the 1877 rules:

No servant of the Club will be employed by any Member to clean clothes, boots or shoes, or to assist him in dressing. No servant of any Member will be allowed to go into any other room than the Dressing room, and then only to assist his master in dressing.

March 27, 1878:

The member is informed that the Steward since July last has been accustomed to charge 40 cents for a joint when twice taken at dinner. . . . The Committee have requested the Steward to deduct 15 cents from the member's bill. The Committee beg to inform the member that the tariff for joints if taken twice has been raised from 25 cents to 35 cents.

September 9, 1885:

A complaint having been made with regard to the size of wine glass used for measuring whiskey etc., the glass being produced it was condemned as being too small and the Steward to be requested for the future to use a fair-sized wine glass.

December 16, 1885:

An inventory of the Club crockery having been taken, it was found there were 201 articles short, and it was decided that the Steward be charged with the shortage.

February 4, 1886:

A discrepancy appearing between the amounts paid by the card players to the waiter, and the amount received in the Bar, the waiter Joe Hughes being called on to explain and admitting that he had received moneys from the card players in excess of what he paid over, it was resolved by the Committee that the services of the waiter Hughes be forthwith dispensed with.

June 2, 1886:

A complaint was received from a member with regard to the luncheon served on the 1st instant. The Secretary was requested to write the member disapproving of the language he used and also informing him that after looking at the bill of fare for the said meal and inquiring of others who partook of same they cannot see cause for complaint.

June 18, 1886:

The Secretary having reported neglect of duty on the part of the Steward last evening, the Committee expressed their disapproval of his conduct, and while delaying action in disposing of the matter, the Committee desired the Secretary to inform him of their strong disapprobation. . . .

The Secretary has instructed to have the following advertisement inserted in the *Halifax Chronicle*, *Montreal Star* and *Toronto Mail*: Wanted a competent and responsible person to take the position of Steward or Manager of the Rideau Club, Ottawa.

August 26, 1886:

The charge for dinner to be for the future 60 cents a head each person dining having the run of the Bill of Fare (dessert to be extra).

September 8, 1886:

A complaint received from Mr Ferguson with regard to charge for dinner was read. The Secretary was instructed to write to Mr Ferguson informing him that it was recently decided to have a club dinner at 60 cents per head which the Committee are not at present inclined to change.

October 6, 1886:

The Steward was spoken to with regard to complaint made by servants as to the manner in which he treated them. Steward J. Parker was instructed to keep on as good terms as possible with the servants consistent with discipline.

January 5, 1887:

A letter was read from the waiters, Chandler and Hamblin, complaining of the manner in which they were treated by the Steward. The Secretary reported that Mr Parker was unfit for duty, owing to being the worse of liquor, on Monday last.

January 6, 1887:

Mr Parker upon being called in handed to the President his resignation which was accepted. Mr R. Inglis was engaged as Steward. Chandler and Hamblin applied for an increase in pay and were given $5.00 a month.

May 4, 1887:

Complaints were received with regard to poker playing being indulged in in the Club. Burroughs and Watt billiard table purchased in Montreal for $630.

May 16, 1887:

A requisition in the complaint book signed by several members was read, asking the Committee to replace the carom billiard table in its former place in the billiard room. It was resolved to replace it as asked and to store the old English table in the Club storeroom. [The minutes for May 9, 1888, state: Resolved to offer the carom billiard table to the Ottawa Club for $150.]

June 6, 1887:

It was resolved that a contract be entered into with Messrs Slattery Bros., to supply the choicest selected meats to the Club for one year at the rate of eleven cents per pound.

August 26, 1887:

Mr R. Inglis resigned as Steward to join the Canadian Anthracite Coal Company. Mr T. Simms hired.

January 14, 1888:

The Steward complained that Mr T.H. Allen had ordered two dishes not on the Bill of Fare when dining in the Club on 11 January, viz: Broiled Smelts and Stewed Apples, and after having said dishes cooked for him, he refused to pay for same as extra dishes. The Secretary was directed to inform Mr Allen that unless he paid for said dishes, the Committee would be obliged to take cognizance of his conduct.

June 6, 1888:

Letter read from Mr C.R. Hall complaining of conduct of waiter Edward Harris. It was resolved that he be dismissed.

June 13, 1888:

The decision to sell the "Prince of Wales" dinner set is rescinded. That set of china to be withdrawn from use except on special occasions.

September 12, 1888:

The Steward laid a charge against the bellboy, Richard Bird, of forging members' names to credit cards and taking the money paid for same. The Steward was instructed to dismiss him at once and get a man to replace him.

March 27, 1889:

A letter was read from Mr R.C. Douglas stating that he doubts the legality of the election of the President at the annual general meeting held on the 20th instant. The Secretary was instructed to write Mr Douglas and inform him that according to the minutes the election was in order and that Mr Sheriff Sweetland was legally elected the President for the year 1889-90.

April 10, 1889:

The Steward suggested that owing to the difficulty in obtaining trained waiters in Canada, that he be permitted to write to England and have two sent out here. It was resolved that his request be sanctioned, with the understanding that the Club be put to no expense whatever beyond engaging them from their arrival in Ottawa for six months at $20 a month.

April 24, 1889:

A complaint was made that recently waiter Jones turned off the gas at the meter a few minutes after one o'clock, notwithstanding that he had been requested to wait until the completion of a rubber then in progress in card room. The Steward was instructed not to have the gas extinguished at one o'clock a.m., but to report the names of all members in the Club after 1.15 a.m.

May 22, 1889:

Information was laid before the meeting that Poker was still played in the Club notwithstanding the view expressed and vote taken at the special General Meeting on 30th May, 1887. After a long discussion the Secretary was instructed to inform those members who were known to have recently played the game in the Club "that a complaint to such effect was before the Committee, and that unless they desisted in breaking this rule, that the Committee would be compelled to take action in the matter."

From the Club constitution, 1889:

Politics and religious questions of every kind shall be absolutely excluded from open discussion in the Club.

. . . [I]f any member shall be guilty of conduct unbecoming a gentleman, the Committee may recommend such member to resign.

No strangers to be shown into the Club Sitting Room, but if accompanied by a member they may be taken into the room known as the Strangers' and Waiting Room.

No stranger shall be admitted into the Clubhouse except on business, and the servants are strictly prohibited from receiving visitors or followers. No member shall give and no servant shall receive a gratuity in the Club on any account whatever.

Servants while on duty will not talk to each other except on matters connected with their business, and no servant is permitted to address an individual member in the house on matters personal or relative to the concerns of the Club.

December 4, 1889:

It was resolved that in view of the present strike in Havana, that it was not advisable to sell cigars by the box. . . .

Also that playing cards are to be paid for both at afternoon and evening sittings by all players. The interpretation of the rule by those who refuse to pay for cards more than once in the same day being entirely in error. No member to be charged more than 25 cents for the use of cards at a single sitting.

February 19, 1890:

The Secretary was instructed to charge Mr R. Dixon Patterson $3.00 for replacing glass in the lavatory door.

June 4, 1890:

No meal to be served in the dining room to cost less than 25 cents. Dumbwaiter with whistle to be installed.

June 11, 1890:

The sum of $25 was voted to the widow of our late billiard marker Alfred Murphy, who died suddenly yesterday.

July 2, 1890:

In view of Mr Clemow having refused to reduce the price of gas, it was resolved to put into the Club the new system of electric light. . . .

The Steward was authorized to engage a billiard marker at $20 a month, and also to replace assistant cook with kitchenmaid, promoting the present kitchenmaid to head maid at $12 a month.

July 24, 1890:

Regarding the insubordination of John Lanahan, hall porter, it was resolved that he be suspended until August 1, on which date he will report himself for duty and apologize to the Steward.

September 11, 1890:

The Secretary reported that the cost of lighting the Club by electricity was treble the previous outlay for gas. Mr Ahearn being called in and given the facts, was asked to light the Club at a fixed rate per annum — he promised to endeavour to meet the wishes of the Club. Meanwhile, a cheaper rate is offered by the Chaudière Electric Light and Power Company, and accepted.

November 5, 1890:

The dining room loss is running at the rate of $50 a month, but it was resolved that as the 60 cents dinner has given such general satisfaction, it would be inadvisable to make any change.

November 19, 1890:

Mrs E.M. Jones asked that she be paid five cents a pound extra for butter from Nov. 1 to May 1 each year. She was informed that the cost at present, with freight, was 39 cents a pound, which the Committee considered high. She agreed to continue the old contract rate.

January 7, 1891:

Gray the billiard marker applied for an increase of pay of $5.00 a month, which was not granted.

February 11, 1891:

Mr E.C. Douglas complained he was not permitted to have bottles brought him from the bar in order to mix his liqueur to his own taste, and suggesting a liqueur stand be purchased in order that the waiters can bring liqueurs for members to mix themselves. It was resolved to allow liqueurs to be taken out of the bar whenever a member expresses a wish to mix his liqueur himself.

July 30, 1891:

No tender having been received from the Chaudière Electric Light and Power Co., it was resolved that the lighting of the Club be returned to the Standard Electric Light Co., Messrs Soper and Ahearn having been notified. The Chaudière Company President, Mr Noel, said he did not think they had been fairly treated by the Club, and asking that their various cutouts and shade holders be returned to the company, as their property.

March 23, 1892:

A recommendation was made by the Steward to increase the pay of Mrs Crowl, the laundress, who has extremely hard work to perform in hot and crowded conditions and who is a very honest reliable woman. It was resolved to increase her pay five dollars a month during the parliamentary session, and install a fan in the laundry in summer. . . .

Receipts from billiards in March, $59.15. Dining room profit, $23.25.

And under the date of July 27, 1892:

A letter was read in reply to one sent the mayor on the 15th July with regards to the squeaking of the electric cars, when rounding the curve opposite the club. We asked that some way be found to compel the Electric Car Co. to prevent this nuisance.

After discussion it was resolved to appoint a deputation of members of the Club to wait upon the president and other officers of the Electric Road, and lay before them the feeling that existed amongst the members of the Club with regard to the loud screeching.

September 7, 1892:

The deputation had waited upon the officers of the Electric Road, who had met them in a fair way, and had promised to use some means in future to stop the noise complained of.

December 21, 1892:

Resolved that Mrs Lamondre, now head housemaid at $10 a month, be paid $4.00 a month extra to clean the new flat.

October 16, 1900:

The Secretary was instructed to write a letter of thanks to the A.D.C. in Waiting thanking His Excellency for his present of wild duck.

1901:

A general discussion took place, with reference to the powers of the Committee, to prevent Members introducing guests to meals, etc., who were, for any reason, likely to prove objectionable to the Members of the Club.

It was agreed to propose certain changes in the Constitution, which would give the Committee discretionary powers in such cases.

1902:

. . . His Royal Highness [the Prince of Wales] has much pleasure in consenting to become an Honorary Member of the Rideau Club, Ottawa.

1912:

Honorary membership has been accepted by His Majesty the King.

1918:

The following named committee has been appointed for the collection, arrangement and presentation of art and memorabilia: Hon. W.L. Mackenzie King, C.M.G., convener.

1934:

The charge for the playing of Mah Jong or Chess for the afternoon or evening shall be ten cents for each player.

Any member who shall be expelled shall forever thereafter be ineligible to be re-admitted as a member of the Club.

1952:

By reason of the cessation of publication of the morning *Citizen*, it was decided that the 5 o'clock *Journals* be increased from 6 to 8, and morning *Gazettes* from 4 to 6.

[Under the terms of a resolution adopted at the annual general meeting on April 9, 1952, Parliamentary Membership was abolished.]

1953:

A notice to be placed over the television set advising members that the set must be turned off at midnight each evening.

September 14, 1953:

The Manager reported difficulty in obtaining full-time waitresses and pantrymaids at the present rate of pay, $65 per month, and approval was given to increasing the basic monthly wage for these two categories to $75 per month.

The Manager reported that Mr C. Fraser Elliott had forwarded some kangaroo meat to the Club and he was directed to inform him that the Committee suggested he take home a portion of the shipment and try it out and if satisfactory give a party at the Club where it could be cooked.

It was decided that a "game dinner" for members only be held some time the latter part of November and that the kangaroo meat be included in the menu, Mr Tolmie being delegated to arrange for the supply of game meat.

It was decided that the prices of Club dinners be increased as follows: With fish course, from $2.10 to $2.35; without fish course, from $1.95 to $2.10.

June 29, 1954:

All luncheon and bell girls on part time, at present receiving $40 per month, to be increased by $5 per month.

Reciprocal relations declined with the City Club, Halifax, but accepted with the Travellers Club, London.

December 21, 1956:

Special parties were being held by Dept. of External Affairs at which no member of the Club was present. Also, a complaint that business meetings were being held in the reading room and the main lounge. Following notice posted: "Members are reminded that it is not in accord with the customary Club practice that the rooms designated for social purposes (main dining room, lounges, reading room and card rooms) be used for business meetings where portfolios, papers, etc. are displayed. Should one be available, a private room may be reserved under the usual conditions on application to the Stewardess."

Complaints received from members of boisterous conduct of guests at a private party, a letter to be sent requesting no recurrence.

April 29, 1958:
Mr Norman MacLeod objected to Soviet ambassador and his counsellor obtaining privileged membership. He was informed they were eligible. Both duly elected.

1959:
Every precaution to cut off noise from the bedroom section is to be taken by the cleaning section, but the offending member is to be advised by letter that there must be no further interference with the cleaning staff in the performance of their duties.

1964:
A complaint by letter was made by Mr J.W. Hughson regarding a shortage of lead pencils in the card room and alleged rudeness on the part of the Card Room maid. It was turned over to the House Committee for any necessary action.

1966:
It was agreed that the Club would not have any special project for the Centennial Year as the outside of the building had been cleaned in 1966.

1967:
The Committee agreed that the Flag should be raised daily during centennial year.

1968:

The question of the notice board in the main washroom was discussed and it was decided that the board would remain but notices would not be posted.

The Secretary reported that it was possible to purchase books of stamps for the city parking lots on Metcalfe between Queen and Albert Streets. These stamps are valued at 30 cents each and each stamp is good for one hour of parking. Regular parking rates in these lots are 35 cents for the first half hour, 25 cents for the second half hour, and 35 cents for subsequent hours. The Committee agreed that the Club should purchase a supply of these stamps and underwrite the first hour of parking in an attempt to encourage more members to use the Club at noon hour.

July 20, 1972:

The suggestion that the Board of Directors wear identification tags when meeting the new Members was not too well received by the Directors present. Instead, it was recommended that the Members of the Board of Directors wear their Club Ties as a means of identification.

May 16, 1974:

Minutes note: "We may be leaving the premises." Nine guests for the May dance, 36 people in all. Event cancelled, and orchestra paid off at $50.

New Members not automatically charged for the 1965 Club history, but advised it is available at $4.50.

The salutation "Esq." to be discontinued, and the Secretary to arrange for new addressograph plates.

June 20, 1974:

No corporate membership for City of Ottawa after request denied for 25 signing privileges.

July 18, 1974:

Membership well below the ceiling of 600, so no urgency to raise the ceiling to 700. Approach suggested to local merchants to see if they are interested in joining.

Attendance by members is on the decline to 10 to 12 on Saturdays.

July 3, 1975:

A complaint was received from Mr A.J. Philips that he was unable to gain entry to the Club on July 1st though he saw people on the veranda. Since the Club was closed there was no hall porter on duty and no one heard Mr Philips ring the bell; several staff members were watching the fireworks.

October 21, 1976:

It was suggested members of the Club who are under 35 might be given an expense allowance from the Club to use in entertaining prospective members at Club functions.

"But Let the Women in Your Lives"

[Henry Higgins, *My Fair Lady*]

uthbert Scott was a
man's man, if ever there was one, and a lady's man, too.
Horseman, fisherman, raconteur, handsome, debonair, it
seemed that nothing could faze him until, as President of
the Rideau Club, he descended the great main staircase on
a 1972 afternoon and passed through the lobby onto
Wellington Street to meet the protesters who were
picketing the Club.

It was a most unusual demonstration, against a very
old and deep-set prejudice, the idea that men were superior
to women, and that women's place was in the home. Or, if
not in the home, certainly not in the Club. Deployed on
the sidewalk, before the overhanging balcony of the white-
walled clubhouse, were portable tables, topped by imitation
linen and plates of thinly cut watercress and cucumber
sandwiches, along with jugs of iced tea.

Earlier that day, the Club had been the scene of a
luncheon for delegates to a Canada-United States policy
conference, and two of the American delegates, Jane
Caskey and Christiane Verdon, had been refused admission
to the premises. The protesters, amid all the media hoopla

that placards and cameras could create, were serving the Misses Caskey and Verdon with sandwiches and tea, while shouting taunts at Club members who crossed their picket line.

Cuthbert Scott's usual charm was lost on the ladies, who shouted him down. He retreated, red-faced, into the clubhouse while the women finished their demonstration, folded their tables and marched on the offices of Treasury Board President Bud Drury, demanding that the government stop patronizing the Rideau Club because it discriminated against women.

Drury refused the demand, but the Club was subjected to a barrage of negative publicity. This caught the eye of Prime Minister Pierre Trudeau and of a member of his cabinet, the Honourable Jeanne Sauvé, and contributed to their antipathy towards the Rideau Club.

President Scott called an emergency meeting of the Club's Board of Directors to consider the unfavourable publicity the Club was getting. He warned that the government was under pressure from the "Women's Lib" movement, and from the parliamentary opposition, to exclude the Club from any government-sponsored functions. Such a boycott, he said, "could have a serious effect on our revenue."

The Board was unmoved, and Vice-President E.D. Lafferty, destined to follow Mr Scott into the presidency, said all members were aware of the rules and regulations regarding the attendance of women in the Club; he maintained that the member responsible for inviting the women luncheon guests (a member of the United States Embassy staff) should receive a strong letter of reprimand from the Secretary.

President Scott recommended that regulations be changed to the extent that ladies be allowed to attend private luncheons in either of the private dining rooms on the first floor. Mr Lafferty insisted the offending member should be reprimanded before any other action was taken.

The minutes recount:

At this point, the Steward entered the room and handed a letter to the President which had just been delivered by hand from the United States Embassy. The letter was from Mr Adolph W. Schmidt, the United States ambassador, expressing the regret of the Ambassador and the Officers of the Embassy for any part they had had in causing the publicity and resulting embarrassment to the Club by a possible oversight on their part.

The Vice President then said that in his view the Ambassador's letter rendered it unnecessary to take any action against the member of the Embassy staff who had invited the ladies to lunch.

It was the beginning of the final phase of a fight that very nearly put the Rideau Club out of business — a phase that would last seven years, amid bitter arguments that sound prehistoric to today's ears but that caught the Club in the full flood of the feminist movement of the 1970s and put it in the van of the equal rights achievements of the 1980s.

One month after the Wellington Street tea party, President Scott reported that only two members had criticized the inclusion of lady guests at luncheons in either of the private dining rooms. The President was instructed to reply to these critics "in suitable terms". For the comfort of women luncheon guests, one of the men's washrooms on the first floor was designated for their use with a "Ladies" sign hung on the door. After this was done, one of the older male members of the Club was making his accustomed use of those facilities when a woman emerged from one of the cubicles, causing him to turn from his work at the wall. Unperturbed, he turned back, finished his business, zipped himself up and tottered from the room, muttering: "Good God!" The incident entered Club legend, but the reactions of the woman concerned are unrecorded.

At the post-tea party Board meeting, President Scott reported a conversation he had had with Mr Norman Smith, publisher of the *Ottawa Journal*, regarding an editorial that appeared in that newspaper during the tea-party protest. The President took the view that the papers ought not to write editorials on matters concerning private clubs. Mr Smith, though a devoted clubman himself, said clubs, like everything else in these changing times, were fair game for comment. The minutes conclude, dryly and wryly, that "the majority of the directors who expressed themselves were inclined to favour Mr Smith's views rather than those of the President."

Women had come a long way, but there was still a way to go, and all the arguments of the equality movement would echo from the hallowed walls, including the voices of wives who were happier to have husbands relaxing in an all-male clubhouse, fishing lodge or stag party, than in mixed company.

Stories are legion regarding the continuing struggle for the admission of women. As recalled by R.A.J. Phillips, in the late 1950s

> Lester Pearson, then Secretary of State for External Affairs, tendered a government luncheon at the Rideau Club for Auguste Lindt, United Nations High Commissioner for Refugees. Agnes Ireland, the External Affairs officer concerned with refugees, was among the guests, but as she entered with Lindt, the porter grasped her firmly by the arm and marched her back down the stairs.
>
> In 1964, MPs Pauline Jewett and Margaret Konantz received similar treatment when they were invited to a luncheon for U.N. Secretary-General U Thant. Escorted out through the kitchen, the two eminent ladies declined the offer of a sandwich "to go" and returned hungry to the House of Commons. Within the hour, External Affairs Minister Paul Martin tendered profuse apologies. The Rideau Club did not apologize.

The issue of women's rights was first raised in the Club in 1921, 57 years after the founding. The man who raised the issue was Mr d'Arcy Scott, who moved what was, for its time, an outrageously daring motion, signalling the advent of the hems-up, boyish bob, rolled-down-hose, roaring twenties:

That it is desirable that a ladies dining room be established in the room at present rented to the Government in the Northwest corner of the ground floor of the Club building.

Consideration of this hot potato was deferred for consultation. Mr Scott tried again a year later. In 1922, he moved "that it is desirable that a ladies dining room be established in the Club building". The resolution was seconded by Major E.F. Newcombe.

The minutes then state:

In amendment, it was moved by Mr A.E. Fripp, K.C., and seconded by Mr Clarence Jameson, that the matter of the establishment of a ladies dining room be referred to the incoming Committee for a report at the next Annual General Meeting. On a standing vote being taken the amendment was declared carried.

In 1923, the largest turnout of members in the Club's history gathered to consider the deferred motion for a ladies' dining room, and that same Mr Fripp opened proceedings by moving that Sir Robert Borden, the former Prime Minister of Canada, be elected President. The motion carried, whereupon Mr Scott's motion came before the meeting.

The minutes:
The Chairman called upon the Secretary to read the report of the Special Committee appointed . . . to consider the establishment of a Ladies Dining Room, which report stated that the establishment of such a department in any way that would be considered satisfactory to the Members and creditable to the Club was not

feasible. It was then moved by Mr J.G.A. Creighton, C.M.G., K.C., and seconded by Colonel D.T. Irwin, C.M.G., that the report . . . be received and adopted.

And that was the end of the matter for 27 years.

It was not until 1950 that this amendment to the constitution was passed:

> Any member may entertain ladies to dinner or refreshments on any evening after such hour as the committee may from time to time determine, but any such guests shall be admitted only to such parts of the Club as may from time to time be determined by the committee.

The snorts could be heard for miles, but there would be no going back.

In 1954, it was suggested that the Club permit the holding of monthly luncheon meetings of the officials of the Federal District Commission in the private dining room, but it was considered that "this would involve the introduction of ladies to the Club at an earlier hour than at present and would not be feasible."

In 1961, a subcommittee was asked to explore with naval architect Captain John B. Roper "the possibility of converting the ground floor premises now occupied by Air Industries, Ltd., into a dining room for members and wives for lunch, dinner and supper." The following year Roper produced plans and sketches for the proposed dining lounge and gave the committee a breakdown of the approximate total cost of about $40,000 plus a sum of $10,000 for improvements considered necessary in the basement which would be done more conveniently at the same time.

In May of 1963, the Ladies Lounge opened, with its own doorway on Wellington Street. There was a controlled passageway into the main part of the building, through which only men could pass.

This "breakthrough" pleased some men and women and angered others. Wives and daughters of members liked it most, having the run of the place with signing privileges on husbands' or fathers' accounts. Professional women went elsewhere.

In 1970, the chairman of the House Committee referred to a letter from the Ladies' Committee and noted that they neglected to refer to themselves as the "Ladies' Advisory Committee". He said that in order to avoid any misunderstanding in the future they should always be referred to as the "Ladies' Advisory Committee", since their terms of reference specifically referred to the operation of the "ladies' section".

The Ladies' Advisory Committee asked permission to set up a special limited ladies' membership, to be called associate members of the ladies' section. In the challenging document, the women had submitted "recommendations to the Men's Committee from the Ladies' Committee." Equal rights? What cheek!

With President Lester B. Pearson in the chair, a general meeting agreed that the Ladies' Advisory Committee be given about a year to see if they could improve the usage of the ladies' section without this new category of membership.

In 1971, President Pearson agreed to a suggestion that a separate menu should be prepared for lunch in the ladies' section, "since the present selection was considered to be too heavy a meal for the Ladies."

In 1974, a letter was received from Dr Michael Oliver, President of Carleton University, in which he stated that his main reason for not using the Rideau Club to entertain was because of the Club's policy towards lady guests. He suggested that the legal position regarding the Ontario Human Rights Code be investigated.

Dr Oliver was advised that, contrary to his comment that he was unable to entertain mixed colleagues in the Club, the Club had facilities to entertain ladies for mixed luncheons in the private dining rooms, the ladies' section of the Club, and upstairs any time after 4 p.m.

After the 1972 expropriation of the premises brought the Club officially within the Parliamentary precinct and made the federal government the Club's landlord, pressures continued to mount.

The federal government, spurred by Prime Minister Trudeau and the expanding number of women senators and MPs, took its business elsewhere and contributed to the decline of the Rideau Club, whose membership was shrinking and whose coffers were in as bad a state of repair as the building itself.

In February of 1978, *The Canadian Press* carried this report:

> Communications Minister Jeanne Sauvé appears to be making little progress in her attempt to stop government employees from spending public money at the Rideau Club, Ottawa's most exclusive haven for affluent men.
>
> Sauvé has nothing against overstuffed armchairs, cigar smoke and brandy. But she is opposed to public servants fattening expense accounts in places which bar women from becoming members. . . .
>
> Sauvé . . . says she "will never put my foot in the place."

And the *Ottawa Citizen* added:

> She went on to say that she could see no reason not to use "economic arguments to fight this form of discrimination of which women are the victims in places like the Rideau Club."

The Club handed the federal government a weapon in that same year, 1978, when it accepted the expropriation advance of $400,000 for the renovation of the premises, having obtained an assurance of continued tenancy when the government shelved plans to build a matching Parliamentary Block on the site.

Having taken "the Queen's Shilling", as it were, the Club found itself enmeshed in the new federal human rights codes, which ban discrimination on federal property. The fat, so to speak, was in the feminist fire.

The Club closed for renovations in 1978, but the minds of some members began to open to the desirability, indeed the necessity, of full membership for women.

A study commissioned in 1978 by that year's President, James Ross, indicates some of the agonies, real or imagined, the members went through on the issue of women's membership in the face of the boycott by the Trudeau government.

"It is assumed," said a report written by Roger Rowley, "that if the Club is to create a ladies membership the government's attitude would change, and further that it would withdraw the sanctions it now imposes."

It went on:

Research indicates that no other Gentlemen's Club of any consequence in the country has ever contemplated making such a dramatic change in the character of what, up until now, has been recognized as a "Town Club", exclusively male in character. We will be breaking new ground, making history and, as we are probably Canada's best known and most important Club, we will be setting an example and establishing precedent.

The decision to welcome ladies as members on an equal footing will be a bold one. If the decision is taken, we must go all the way, with no holdbacks or reservations. The transition must be carried out with class and dignity . . . the Club is well known for its low public relations profile and for its reticence and its problems in dealings with the press.

Any radical change in the status of the Rideau Club will be a news item of national, if not of international importance.

It would seem sensible for the President, or a member nominated by him, to discuss the whole question privately with H.E. the Governor General, the Prime Minister and possibly other selected senior members of the government and the judiciary.

If ladies are extended membership privileges the board should keep an eye to the numbers joining because in theory there should be as many memberships available to ladies as there are to gentlemen. . . .

The sanctity of the Billiard Room is recognized. The threat of a takeover of the tables by the distaff side seems minimal, since very few Ottawa ladies are thought to be avid players of billiards, snooker or pool. We should not forbid a lady to approach the tables. . . .

Ladies should be given executive and administrative appointments in relation to their numbers vis-à-vis gentlemen.

We must know when and if the Government plans to bring down new legislation on discrimination. We must act before the Government makes its move.

Such a policy will cause dismay, anguish and distress to some of our members. Some gentlemen may be angry enough to resign. One of the great bastions of male security, freedom, seclusion and social companionship will go. There will no longer be a place for "man talk" in a totally protected male atmosphere. There will be no place to "get away from it." All this will disappear.

But we will take a big step into the new social order and thereby protect ourselves for the present and the future, from pressure and abuse.

We will be leading the way in meeting the demands of Canadian women that they be accepted fully into a free social democracy.

Membership should increase and hence improve our financial position while increasing Club usage.

On November 22, 1978, a special general meeting
was called to consider the admission of "ladies" to full and
equal membership, and this attracted an even larger crowd
than had the meeting in 1923.

Author and Club member Shirley Woods, in his
book *Ottawa: The Capital of Canada*, recalls:

> The lightest moment of the evening occurred when a
> well-known journalist, who was an ardent advocate of
> the motion, reminded his fellow members that the
> Liberal government would not entertain at the Rideau
> Club because of its "discrimination". Shaking with
> emotion, he begged his audience to reflect on this sad
> state of affairs, and harking back to the club's founder
> (Sir John A. Macdonald), he finished with the question,
> "What would Sir John say?"
>
> There was a brief silence and then a voice answered,
> "Vote Tory!"

I was that journalist, and what Woods neglects to
mention was his own impassioned speech to the meeting,
urging that the Club did not need transitory politicians or
mandarins (or, presumably, journalists), and that Old
Ottawans were the men with the real stuff.

Woods develops the point in his book:

> It is . . . well to remember that Parliamentarians are for
> the most part transients who have little or no effect upon
> the city. A few Prime Ministers, notably Sir John A.
> Macdonald, Sir Wilfred [sic] Laurier, and the Right
> Honourable Lester B. Pearson, have been permanent
> residents of stature. And those who run the government
> departments, the Mandarins, have no more *direct* influ-
> ence on the people of Ottawa than they do on the

citizens of Moose Jaw, Saskatchewan, or Truro,
Nova Scotia.

Having thus spoken, like the son and grandson of
Rideau Club forebears, Woods retired from the field, and
eventually from the Club. Four months later, a less impassioned general meeting on March 28, 1979, voted to admit
women to full membership but, alas for Major General
Rowley's projection, five months passed before the name of
any woman came forward in nomination.

The *Ottawa Journal* reported that "women who suc-
cessfully battled for full membership rights at the Rideau
Club are staying away in droves. . . ."

Sylvia Gelber, a Labour Canada special adviser who
had been prominent in the tea-party picket eight years
before, explained why none of the protesting women had
applied: it wasn't that they were seeking admittance, it was
the principle of the thing.

"We were concerned as taxpayers," she said, "that the
federal government was spending a considerable amount of
money for business lunches and meetings at a club where
discrimination was practised."

One week after Mrs Jean Pigott became the first
woman member, the Club burned down. (Wags of the time
said it was the illustrious Mrs Pigott burning her bra.)

The presence of women altered the atmosphere of the
Rideau Club, in its temporary refuge in the Chateau
Laurier and finally in the new penthouse quarters, which

veered away from macho decor into the spectacular place it is. Women were more in evidence as guests than as members, but their numbers grew gradually, though they grew to nothing near the parity envisaged in the Rowley forecast.

The same reluctance was evidenced by the politicians, who showed little disposition to use the Club, even after the government of the day, satisfied that all the federal anti-discrimination laws had been met, lifted its ban. The government had taken its eating, drinking and meeting business elsewhere, chiefly to the feeding troughs and watering holes that existed on Parliamentary and government premises, and political partisans had acquired a tendency to gather in acceptable bistros downtown. It was the men and women of the business and professional community who flocked to the Rideau Club, along with visiting firemen who found the Club an agreeable place to gather; and they joined in such numbers that solvency was achieved.

What, to re-ask my earlier question, would founding father Sir John A. think?

He would be surprised, but perhaps not displeased, at the number of women present. He might note the tendency of men to congregate in the bar, the Reading Room and around the billiard tables (no restriction, mind you — just a tendency).

He would certainly deplore the absence of the politicians on a day-in, night-out basis, since that is what he founded the Club for in the first place. But considering the number of drinking places available in downtown Ottawa and environs, he might not feel deprived, even though only beer and wine are available in the Parliamentary restaurants. (He would approve the fact that every Parliamentary office has a fridge, along with virtually every other appliance known to man or woman.)

If not the politicians, he might ask, who makes Ottawa and the Rideau Club go?

The answer seems to be that the capital city has developed a life of its own, even though it continues to be a company town, the company being the federal government. As architect Tim Murray put it, "as long as the smoke keeps coming out of the Peace Tower smokestack, we are in business."

Not many would share author Shirley Woods' Old Ottawa scorn of politicians, but it is a fact that they do not rank high on the totem pole of citizen esteem; they tend to keep to themselves on the Ottawa scene, elite and otherwise.

We close with a salvo unleashed against politicians by the aforementioned Hamilton Southam, in a 1989 paper read before the Royal Society, complaining that governments had stopped taking the advice of the cultural elite.

Mr Southam, an eloquent defender of elitism "provided I am permitted to define the term", argued that "[i]n an age where our other elites are flexing their muscles, our political elites are quaking in their boots, even showing the early signs of paranoia."

His prescription:

> Our political masters are spending vast sums on polling and studying *us*. The time has come for *us* to study *them*. . . .
>
> It should start with the collection of extremely detailed personal information about the people who compose it . . . date and place of birth, racial and cultural background, education, and places of residence between birth and election. We should have a brief sketch of such places, indicating whether he has a rural, small town or urban background. We should know the languages he speaks, or are spoken around him, his business or profession, his income and the sources thereof, his credit rating. We should know about his health, marital status and children, . . . tastes and interests, i.e., is he into sports (what sports?) or books (what books?) or music (what music?)?
>
> This is the sort of information our political masters would require of us if we sought to enter their service. Why should we not ask it of them as they seek to enter ours? . . .
>
> [T]oo many are now attracted to Parliament by the lure of TV and the take-home pay. They lack the training and self-confidence to belong to the political or indeed any elite. They replace expertise and ideas . . . by counting noses. For doing that they seem over-paid.

That formula is not unlike the one the Rideau Club used to apply to nominees for membership, in the days when just about every member of the Club knew just about every other member, and new people were judged by the likelihood, or not, that they would fit in. Today's larger membership is more impersonal, even if the process of selection is more democratic, not to say less elitist.

The word "elite" is one often applied to clubs like the Rideau Club, usually in a pejorative sense by non-members. Few club people bother to mount a defence, perhaps aware of the pitfall of sounding pompous, silly, or fat-headed, or all of the above. Hamilton Southam has no such qualms, bewailing what he calls "the massification of our elites", and calling for "the elitification of the masses".

A Club history is not the place in which to elaborate on Hamilton Southam's theme, but it is worth dwelling upon if we are to regard club people as achievers, rather than creatures of privilege, snobs or spoiled brats. The lifting of the curtains that used to shroud the doings of the Rideau Club has not opened its gates to all — the dues and fees would see to that in any case, and the needy needn't apply. Politicians, as we have seen, do not care to apply, but women, increasingly, do. Their presence has done more than any other thing to change and brighten the ambience of Club life, and ensure that mustiness, having been banished from the premises, does not set in again.

And that is reason enough to celebrate a 125th birthday.

Appendix

PRESIDENTS OF THE RIDEAU CLUB

The Rt. Hon. SIR JOHN A. MACDONALD	1865-1866
Lt.-Col. HEWITT BERNARD	1867-1868
The Hon. GEORGE W. ALLAN	1869
The Rt. Hon. SIR RICHARD CARTWRIGHT	1870-1871
The Hon. SIR ALEXANDER GALT	1872
JOSEPH M. CURRIER	1873-1878
ALONZO WRIGHT	1879
The Hon. JAMES COCKBURN	1880
THOMAS C. KEEFER	1881
The Hon. WILLIAM A. HENRY	1882-1883
JOHN SWEETLAND	1884-1885, 1888-1890
The Hon. FRANCIS CLEMOW	1886
JOHN A. GEMMILL	1887
HELIER V. NOEL	1891-1892
Col. WALKER POWELL	1893
CHARLES MAGEE	1894-1895
The Hon. SIR GEORGE PERLEY	1896-1897
JOHN CHRISTIE	1898-1899
Col. DE LA CHEROIS T. IRWIN	1900-1901
CHARLES B. POWELL	1902-1903
Dr. FREDERICK MONTIZAMBERT	1904-1905
FREDERICK W. AVERY	1906-1907
JOHN T. LEWIS	1908-1910
DAVID M. FINNIE	1911-1913
ROBERT GILL	1914-1922
The Rt. Hon. SIR ROBERT BORDEN	1923-1924

J.A. JACKSON	1925-1929
Col. CAMERON M. EDWARDS	1930-1931
HAMNETT P. HILL	1932-1934
CHARLES G. COWAN	1935-1936
Col. HENRY C. OSBORNE	1937-1938
OLIVER M. BIGGAR	1939-1941
The Hon. FREDERIC E. BRONSON	1942-1945
KENNETH A. GREENE	1946
DUNCAN K. MacTAVISH	1947-1948
JOHN A. AYLEN	1949-1950
BARRY GERMAN	1951-1952
The Hon. JAMES D. HYNDMAN	1953-1954
CHALMERS J. MACKENZIE	1955-1956
ASCANIO J. MAJOR	1957-1959
Vice-Admiral HAROLD T.W. GRANT	1960-1962
The Hon. DOUGLAS C. ABBOTT	1962-1963, 1968
Rear-Admiral WALLACE B. CREERY	1964-1965
CHARLES G. GALE	1965-1967
A. HARTLEY ZIMMERMAN	1967
A. DAVIDSON DUNTON	1969-1970
The Rt. Hon. LESTER B. PEARSON	1970-1972
CUTHBERT SCOTT	1972-1973
ERNEST D. LAFFERTY	1974-1975
STUART F.M. WOTHERSPOON	1976-1977
JAMES ROSS	1978-1979
GUY ROBERGE	1980-1981
DENIS M. COOLICAN	1982-1983
ANGUS C. MORRISON	1984-1985
Air Marshal HUGH CAMPBELL	1986
WILLIAM H. McMILLAN	1987-1988
DAVID W. SCOTT	1988-1989
The Hon. JOHN J. URIE	1989